Alexa Tewkesbury

Published 2010 by CWR, Waverley Abbey House, Waverley Lane, Farnham, Surrey GU9 8EP, UK. Registered Charity No. 294387. Registered Limited Company No. 1990308.

See back of book for list of National Distributors.
Unless otherwise indicated, all Scripture references are from the Good News Bible, copyright © American Bible Society 1966, 1971, 1976, 1992, 1994.
Concept development, editing, design and production by CWR
Illustrations: Helen Reason, Dan Donovan and CWR
Printed in Finland by WS Bookwell
ISBN: 978-1-85345-553-7

Hello, people! We're Saucy the cat and Gruff the dog, and you're about to discover more about cats and dogs than you probably ever thought possible.

For instance, have you ever wondered what cats get up to late at night when you're in bed and they're out on the prowl? And have you ever asked yourself what dogs dream about when they're sleeping?

Well, this is it – your chance to find out exactly what goes on in our zany world.

Not only that, but living with John and Sarah, we get to hear lots about God. We've realised that although it can sometimes be hard trying to live God's way, God doesn't leave you to struggle on your own. When you give your life to Him, He sends His Holy Spirit to come and live inside you to help you do right things instead of wrong ones. What an amazing present that is – God's power in your life every single day.

So what are you waiting for? Read on – you'll never see dogs and cats in the same way again ...!

HI! WE'RE THE TOPZ GANG

– Topz because we all live at the 'top' of something ... either in houses at the top of the hill, at the top of the flats by the park, even sleeping in a top bunk counts! We are all Christians, and we go to Holly Hill School.

We love Jesus, and try to work out our faith in God in everything we do – at home, at school and with our friends. That even means trying to show God's love to the Dixons Gang who tend to be bullies, and can be a real pain!

If you'd like to know more about us, visit our website at **www.cwr.org.uk/topz** You can read all about us, and how you can get to know and understand the Bible more by reading our 'Topz' notes, which are great fun, and written every two months just for you!

DAY 1

Gruff:

It was just like any other morning. I had breakfast – moist meaty chunks in delicious gravy with a sprinkling of biscuits (which, I have to say, always smells a whole lot more appetising than that funny looking stuff John tips into a bowl and pours milk all over. Still, each to his own, I suppose). I had a good, long scratch – behind the right ear; under the chin; across the tummy. John's mum gave me the usual, 'Stop that Gruff', like she always does. I mean, what is it with people and dogs scratching? Haven't they ever had an itch before? Because, I'm telling you, when you're a dog, if you've got an itch, you've just got to scratch.

Then I had my morning rootle about behind the garden shed. Bit of a squeeze what with the hedge and that rusty old wheelbarrow, but it's kind of my special place and I love it. It's where I keep things.

That's when I heard John calling: 'Gruff!' And I knew it was time. A bit of mad dashing round in circles, then, snap, on went the lead and we were off.

Turn right for the park. The first walk of the day is always in the park. That's where we go, me and John. Without fail. Come rain or shine; snow or howling winds.

It's our time. Our walk. Our spot to do our spot of bonding, dog and boy, boy and dog ... except for the days when we turn left and go towards the shops. Like today.

We go to the shops when John's family runs out of milk or bread or tea bags, or whatever else it is people can't seem to do without first thing in the morning. What they don't seem to realise is that what dogs can't do without first thing in the morning is their run in the park. A trot along the pavement's all well and good but it's nothing compared to the lead coming off and the feel of soft, springy grass under your paws.

I went to turn right, as usual, and John said, 'No, not the park, Gruff. We need milk,' and pulled me the other way. I mean, I should have guessed when he didn't pick up my ball on the way out. I've got to say, I wasn't happy. Not happy in the slightest.

So, I did what I always do when an outing isn't going my way: I dawdled. No park for me, no easy dog walk for John. Well, fair's fair. I dragged my feet; I stopped for a sniffle here; I paused for a snuffle there; I sat down for a scratch; I kept turning my head and looking wistfully over my shoulder. And it worked a treat.

'OK, OK,' John sighed finally. 'I'll get the milk and then we'll go to the park.'

Great stuff. Mission accomplished.

So there I was, tied to the newspaper stand

outside the corner shop while John went in for milk, minding my own business like it's always best to do when left to yourself on the pavement.

And then it happened. Right in front of my very ears and eyes.

From inside the shop, there was a cry of, 'Stop him! He's stolen my bag!' The next thing I knew, a tall man was hurtling through the doorway, looking very red in the face and clutching a large, green handbag. No one seemed to be following, and all of a sudden – I KNEW. This was my moment.

I could see it now. Headline news:

GALLANT GRUFF SAVES THE DAY

(NOT TO MENTION WOMAN'S LARGE, GREEN HANDBAG)

All I had to do to catch the handbag stealer was get free from the newspaper stand. Simple ... or not. I pulled one way, then the other. Nothing doing. I tugged backwards and tried to wriggle out of my collar. Nope, no good.

Nothing for it, then ... I pulled ... and heaved ... and yanked ... and with a

effort (not to mention a bit of a crash as the newspaper stand toppled to one side and hit the pavement, shooting the day's news in all directions at the same time), I was free!

The man was still in sight and I ran and ran; past the bakery (nice smell coming from there, I must admit); past the butcher's (even nicer smell coming from there, but let's face it, some things, like chasing after large, green handbag stealers, are more important than nice smells ... I think ... yes, of course, they are); and past the post office. Lead trailing, I was positively pelting along. This was even better than a run in the park. My legs were pounding that pavement, back and forth, back and forth! Short they may be, but slow they are definitely not.

One final push, then – YESSS! I caught him! Outside the library.

I ran in between his legs and, thwack! Down he went like a ... like a ... well, like a man who's just stolen a large, green handbag

and tripped over a dog. It was awesome.

More than that, I was awesome! I was the hero **of Holly Hill. The magnificent marvel of the moment. Any minute now, John would appear, beaming with pride. He'd unclip my lead, lift me high above his head, and the crowd of onlookers would go wild! I'd be on dog choc treats and fresh sausages for a month ...**

If only I could stop whatever that was prodding my bottom ...

'Gruff! Gruff!'

Was that Saucy? What on earth was she doing outside the library?

'Gruff!' **Saucy hissed once more.** 'You're doing it again. Dreaming. I don't know what it's all about this time but your little legs are going like an express train and it's very distracting. Will you wake up!'

'What?' I was very confused. I wasn't outside the library at all. I was lying on the landing rug. And it wasn't even morning, it was the middle of the afternoon.

'No ...' I murmured. 'I – I've just caught a large, green handbag stealer and I'm a magnificent marvel and I'm about to get choc treats and fresh sausages and I've ... I've ...'

'Been having another dream,' **finished Saucy bluntly.** 'Why can't dogs sleep like cats? Quietly.'

'Gruff!'
'Gruff!'
'Gruff!'

Saucy:

It's always the same with Gruff. One dream and all of a sudden he thinks he should be a superhero – or a champion basketball player; or the first dog to swim the River Thames from end to end; or some very important person's favourite slipper fetcher.

I say to him, 'Gruff, you've been dreaming. That's all it is.'

I warn him about eating leftover cheese sandwiches, but does he take the slightest bit of notice? Apparently not. But then, he's a dog, and as far as I can tell, when it comes to food, dogs are a law unto themselves. They eat anything (and everything). Not like cats. Cats have so much more sense. Some people complain about our eating habits and say we're 'just so fussy'. I prefer to think of it as watching what we eat. I'd sooner be a careful cat than a daft dog any day of the week. I mean, when will Gruff ever learn? He's not designed to eat cheese. It's no wonder he's always dreaming.

Still, I might as well be talking to myself for all the notice he takes of me. It wouldn't be so bad if he woke up, shook himself off and went right back to sleep, but he has one dream and suddenly all he can think about is his 'purpose in life'.

'Perhaps I should be this,' he'll say, then a couple of weeks later, **'Perhaps I should be that'**. You never know what he's going to want to be next. It's so tiring. Not restful at all. Especially in the middle of the afternoon when I'm lying in the hot spot on top of the laundry basket where the sun pours in. I can be trying to snatch a few catch-up winks if I've been out prowling with the girls the night before, and all I can hear is Gruff huffing and puffing about what sort of pet he's meant to be. If only dogs could be more like cats.

I say to him, 'If you were having this conversation with my Sarah, do you know what she'd say? She'd say, "Ask God what He thinks. The most important thing is to be what God wants you to be because He knows what's best for all of us." Which is actually fantastically good advice from any point of view. Dreams are dreams and what's real is real. And you are what you are, Gruff, so will you please stop going on about what you could be and let me sleep.'

But what's Gruff's reply? **'I know dreams are dreams and what's real is real. I happen to be very intelligent, you know. They said so at puppy training – "Very intelligent but with a bit of a wicked streak". (I guess by that they mean that streak of white hair under my tummy, which I have to admit is pretty wicked.) And obviously I am what I am – and the last thing I ever do is go on about it.'**

I've got one thing to say to that:

Pah!

DAY 2

Gruff:

Not that I'm going on about it or anything, because going on about stuff is the last thing dogs ever do. We're far too busy chasing balls and snuffling round dustbins and thinking about food and hanging around waiting for the next walk. I'm telling you, it's endless.

The thing is, though, all this chasing after large, green handbag stealers has got me thinking ... Maybe I should be a guard dog. This house could do with a guard dog. I reckon it could be what I was born for. Let's face it, even my name's got 'guard dog' written all over it –

I mean, if John had called me Floppy or Fluffy, that wouldn't be the same at all. But Gruff, that's a proper guard dog name, that is. It's a sort of cross between a growl and a huff – and let's face it, no one's going to mess with a dog who's growling and huffing, no matter how short his legs are.

Not only that, but I already know what guard dogs do: they **bark** – which is pretty much what I do a lot of anyway.

When someone comes to the door, I **bark.** When the telephone rings, I **bark.** When I hear a door slam, I **bark.** When a floorboard creaks, I **bark**. Actually, with floorboard creaking, I suppose what I make is more of a harrumphing sound, so I might need to step the volume up on that. And I suppose I could always improve my growling – make it last longer; maybe start softly and get louder –

grrrrrrrrrrrrrr!

Wooo! I could even scare myself doing that.

John is going to love this. He'll be able to introduce me to all his friends as 'Guard Dog Gruff'. That'll make everyone take notice. There'll be no more offering my paw or rolling over for a tummy tickle. I shall be striding tall – well, as tall as I can on these little legs – carrying out regular patrols of the house, always on the alert, and generally looking like a dog who is not to be messed with. It's going to be great. I don't know why I never thought of it before. If this doesn't prove to the world (and John in particular) that I am super-charged and super-special, nothing will.

Here I go, head up, ears back, tail just so ... looking good ...

Saucy:

What is that dog doing? I mean, seriously, what does he think he looks like? How is a cat supposed to have the first of her ten-a-day, bottom-of-the-stairs grooming sessions (not one of which can be missed, I'll have you know) with a dog pacing up and down on the rug by the front door? Not only that, but he keeps making a silly sort of growling noise. Well, I say 'growling'. That suggests it might actually frighten somebody. To be quite honest, I've come across mice that sound scarier.

A lot of Gruff's strange behaviour I've learned to ignore. This is something new and I simply can't.

'Gruff! What on earth are you up to this time?'

'What does it look like?' he said.

'If I knew what it looked like, I wouldn't be asking, would I?' I snapped.

'Good point,' he agreed. **'Take a guess.'**

'Do I look like the sort of cat who's got time to sit around playing guessing games?' I said, lifting my head and looking as far down my nose at him as I could. If there's one thing I'm good at, it's being haughty. 'Will you, please, just go away. I'm trying to have my wash.'

Gruff shook his head. **'Can't do that, I'm afraid,'** he said. **'This is my new job.'**

'What new job?'

'This new job,' he said. **'I'm a guard dog.'**

'Says who?'

'Says me.'

'Since when?'

'Since my dream about catching the large, green handbag stealer,' he announced. **'This is it. This is what I was made for.'**

I knew it. I said so, didn't I? One dream and Gruff's away. 'I can be this, I can be that.' Why can't he just be happy with who he is?

More importantly, where's a cat got to go these days to finish her first wash of the day in peace?

DAY 3

Gruff:

Call me an old moaner if you want, but who says living with people is easy? Don't get me wrong. I think they're adorable and all that, and I'd be quite happy to spend all day every day following John's each and every step. But when it comes to understanding dog speak, people just don't get it.

I mean, there I am being a prize guard dog – in other words doing the perfect job for me and doing it perfectly. Along comes the postman, bark bark; up drives the milkman, bark bark; bang goes the back door, bark bark bark; and on and on. I could not have

bark bark bark bark bark bark bark bark

bark bark bark bark

been more ready to take on the world to protect my family.

And what do I get?

'Be quiet, Gruff! That's enough of that racket.'

'Gruff, will you please settle down. Go on, get in the kitchen.'

'What is wrong with you today? Just stop your silly noise!'

Pah! I ask you – SILLY NOISE! There is nothing silly about my bark, let me tell you, and it is most definitely not a noise. How dare they? My bark is a very effective warning system and should not be ignored.

Just to prove the point, I made sure I barked at every tiny sound. I also threw in a few Gruff-special growls to show just how serious (not to mention talented) I am with this whole guard dog business. I was good, too. More than good. I was brilliant.

But did I get doggie chocs or an extra spoonful of moist meaty chunks for my efforts? Did I, dog biscuits. I got sent out in the garden with the door shut firmly behind me where apparently I have to 'stay until I've learnt to behave myself'!

Naturally Saucy thinks it's hilarious. She's up there now, perched on Sarah's bedroom windowsill looking down her nose at me through the glass. Well, two can play at that game. I've got my own perch. In fact, it's better than a perch. It's a hidey-hole and it's all mine. The gateway to another world. No cats allowed ... I'm off behind the shed.

Saucy:

'Psst!'

I hissed. 'You can come out now.'

No answer.

'Gruff?' I said, louder this time. 'You'd better come out from behind the shed. They need you in the house in a minute. They're going out.'

Still there was nothing. No sound at all. I tried to peer under the old wheelbarrow, but what with the hedge and that bit of bramble, there was no way I was going to get my fur dirty squeezing in behind to see where Gruff was. Trust a dog to choose such an awkward place to hide.

I said, 'Gruff, I know you're there so you may as well stop sulking and come on out. You don't want to get into even more trouble.'

There was still no answer, so I put my tail in the air and stalked off. There's just no helping some dogs.

It was odd, though. Gruff had to be there. He certainly wasn't anywhere else. The only place he could be was behind the shed. So why was I left with the curious feeling that he wasn't ...?

DAY 4

Saucy:

I don't like days like this. Nothing feels right because Gruff's in a bad mood. And may I say that doesn't often happen. As much as all his pacing around and barking and growling was as annoying as being given a can of tuna with no tin opener – I am so with the family on that one – now he's all miserable, and somehow that feels even worse. He's been curled up behind the sofa all morning. I can't even see him properly because there's a magazine rack in the way.

I said to him, 'What is your problem, Gruff? They've forgiven you, haven't they? They've let you back in the house. What's with all this lying around and not saying two words to a flea?'

'Don't know why you're asking, you don't really care,' he humphed. **'And even if you did, you wouldn't understand.'**

'I won't understand if you don't tell me, that's for sure,' I said. There's nothing worse than a dog who feels sorry for himself.

'All right, then, if you must know,' he began, **'I wanted to feel special. I thought, I know, I'll do what comes naturally. I'll be a guard dog. And not just any old guard dog. I'll be the best guard dog in Holly Hill. Won't that be a nice surprise for everybody? Well, it might have been a surprise, but it obviously wasn't a nice one.'**

'I don't think it was being a guard dog that was the problem,' I said, as kindly as I could. 'I reckon it was all that barking that did it. A little goes a long way as far as people are concerned. And cats, come to that.'

'But how can you be a guard dog without barking?' he said. **'That would be like being a goldfish and never blowing bubbles.'**

'I'm sure even guard dogs aren't meant to bark when someone shuts the fridge door or snaps the top back on a sandwich box,' I tried to point out. 'Anyway, what do you mean, you wanted to feel special? You're special already, don't you know that?'

Gruff heaved his little shoulders up in a shrug. **'But that's the whole point,'** he sighed. **'I'm not special. I'm not like Sally the Labrador round the corner. She's a guide dog. She looks after a blind man and helps him cross the road, and catch the bus, and go to the shops. I'm not like George the Alsatian who works with the police. He's really important and PC Cropper says he doesn't know where he'd be without him. I'm not even like Pollyanna the Pekinese who keeps winning all those rosettes because she's so beautiful. I'm just small and grey and scruffy. I don't have an important job to do and, worst of all, I'm just so ... ordinary.'**

There was nothing for it. I was going to have to go round the other way and crawl in beside him behind the sofa. You can't have a proper heart to heart when there's a magazine rack between you.

I said, 'You needn't think I'm making a habit of this. You know I'm not one for small spaces.'

Gruff shuffled up a bit to make more room, but I still felt like the filling in a sandwich.

'What I don't think you realise,' I went on, 'is that being ordinary makes you just about as special as you can be. You ask my Sarah, she'll tell you. "In the beginning," she said to me once when she was giving my fur a groom, "God created everyone and everything, and when He'd finished, He looked and saw that it was all good". That means He was pleased with it. My Sarah knows because that's what it says in the Bible and she's always reading it. She says that God's made every living thing exactly the way He wants it to be. He doesn't want you to be like Sally the Labrador or George the Alsatian or Pollyanna the Pekinese. He doesn't want you to try to be like any other dog. He just wants you to be you.

Small, grey, scruffy, ordinary YOU.

That's the you He made. That's the you He can use to do amazing things for Him. That's the you He loves.'

'But I was trying to do something amazing,' moaned Gruff. **'I was trying to be an amazing guard dog.'**

'Yes, and last week you had a dream that you were a sheep dog,' I said, 'so you tried to be one of those. John said you spent your entire morning walk doing your best to round up the pigeons in the park, and they weren't impressed. And the week before that you were running round and round the garden as fast as your little legs could carry you because you'd dreamt you were doing a greyhound race, so you thought you'd try being a greyhound. And the week before that, in another dream, you were in the circus. For hours afterwards you were trying to do tricks like somersaulting off the sofa, and balancing all sorts of different things on the end of your nose – including me, if you remember, and I was not happy about it!

'My Sarah says that God has the best ideas for what we should do and where we should be because He knows us inside out. What we have to do is ask Him to show us. He might not answer straight away but He'll always be there, walking alongside us; letting things unfold bit by bit. We just have to be patient. He can do good things with us and with our lives if we give ourselves to

Him to guide and to lead. More than we ever could do by ourselves.

'So, Gruff,' I finished, 'stop all this trying to be this, that and whatever else it is you've been dreaming about lately and ask God what He wants for you instead. My Sarah says He's always listening. And she should know, she hardly ever stops talking to Him … And speaking of talking, I've said everything I've got to say now, so can we please get out from behind the sofa? I'm so squashed I've got pins and needles in both my back legs and I think my tail's got a kink in it.'

DAY 5

Gruff:

What a morning! Sarah's all in a state because she's just spent 'hundreds of days' (so she says) doing a MASSIVE jigsaw of a baby rabbit sitting on a huge dog's head, and now she's got to the end she's discovered two pieces are missing. She says it's all John's fault because she reckons he was the last person to get it out. John's all in a state because, to get her own back, Sarah's been in his bedroom and emptied all his Lego down the back of his bookcase. And now Saucy's all in a state because Sarah says it's 'impossible growing up in a place like this' and is busy packing up her stuff ready to move in with her best friend, Josie. Honestly, it's like living in a mad house.

I said to Saucy, 'Of course Sarah's not going to move in with Josie. For one thing, you can't just move yourself into someone else's home whenever you feel like it, no matter how

annoying you think your twin brother is or how many pieces of jigsaw he may or may not have lost. There are arrangements to be made. People to tell. I mean, have you heard Sarah on the phone to Josie telling her to get the spare bed ready, because I certainly haven't? Let's face it, Sarah's mum's only just found out and she doesn't look the slightest bit bothered. Believe me, it's not going to happen. It's obviously just one of those storm in a teacup things. And apart from anything else, Saucy, Sarah's never going to leave you.

Saucy:

It's not that I'm not good on my own, because I am actually. I'm as good at being on my own as ants are at living in crowds. It's what cats are, you see. **Strong and independent. Free as air.** It's a known fact. We're born free and we live free. We come and we go however the fancy takes us. That's why we have cat flaps – so that our fancy can take us wherever we choose, whenever we want. All by ourselves.

Of course, I don't mind having the odd night out with the girls. The odd night out not all by yourself can be quite a laugh. We get up to all sorts of mischief after dark. We give ourselves points for fence-running, which involves nimbly tiptoeing your way along the top of all the back garden fences in our street as quickly as you can. If you put a paw wrong you fall off and lose all your points.

Star, the new tortoiseshell kitten who's moved in at the end of the row, lost all hers last Saturday night.

I said to her, 'You've got to take it steady. There's a fishpond in the garden at number 16. The last thing you want to do is end up in there.'

I should know. I did end up in there once. Put me right off fish for quite a while, I can tell you.

We also do bin-lid leaping where we jump from dustbin to dustbin when they've all been put out in a row ready for rubbish collection day.

Sometimes, if we're feeling really adventurous, we scamper along the back alley as far as the chip shop. Then we hide under the benches where people often sit to eat their takeaway, and try to make them jump by rubbing up against their legs just as they've got a mouthful.

Sukie, the Persian from number 12, did a great job one night. The man whose ankles she wrapped herself around shot up from his seat and threw all his chips in the air. It was very funny to watch, but I must admit I felt bad about it for weeks. I kept hoping he had a sandwich tucked away otherwise he would have gone very hungry.

But on the nights we've got nothing planned and it's just me, I don't tend to leave the garden. That's not because I'm nervous or scared of the dark when I'm by myself, oh no, not at all. It's just because I like being in the garden. Close to the cat flap. That way, if Sarah needs me, I can be there quick as a flash. In two shakes of a cat's tail even.

Sarah thinks I spend a lot of nights indoors on her bed, snuggling up against her pillow, because I'm worried about being alone in the dark – which is just nonsense. She tells people I've got NITS (Nearly Impossible To stop Snuggling problems). Well, I agree I like a snuggle. Who doesn't? If it's a choice between the rug on the landing and Sarah's pillow, I'll take the pillow every time.

But, it's like I say, cats are independent. They don't need people the way people need each other. They certainly don't want company the way dogs seem to all the time. Sometimes there's just no getting away from Gruff.

So if I do choose to snuggle up with Sarah when she goes to bed, it's got nothing to do with me needing to be close to her or being nervous of the dark, and everything to do with her not wanting to go to sleep on her own.

Only now Sarah's packing a bag and saying she's going to live with Josie, and I don't know what to do. If Sarah's not here, we won't be able to have our nightly snuggles. Obviously I'll be all right because I'm happy on my own anywhere, any time, but what about Sarah? She'll be somewhere else and her bed here will be empty and lonely and … cold. And her pillow will be, too. And what's the point snuggling up next to an empty, lonely, cold pillow? I mean, where's the comfort in that?

'She's not going anywhere,' Gruff keeps saying **'I know these things. You can trust me, I'm a dog.'**

But if she's not going anywhere, why is her bag still packed? And why is her mum saying, 'What time shall I drop you over there?' And why is she taking her toothbrush …?

Gruff:

So I get things wrong sometimes. Is it my fault if people make crazy decisions based on lost jigsaw puzzle pieces? You'd never catch

a dog behaving like that, that's for sure. There's no point overreacting if someone might possibly have done something you're not happy about.

For instance, if John happened to give me my moist meaty chunks a little later than I was expecting them, would I storm off in a huff? Of course not. I'd just let him know what the time was by sitting and staring sadly into my empty bowl and making this little sort of whimpering sound that I've been practising. I've got it so it works a treat now – as I discovered when I lost my ball under the sofa. One whimper and John and Sarah and their mum came rushing in to see what was wrong. I got my ball back in a jiffy. You see, the thing with people is, it's just a matter of knowing how to handle them.

OK, so I told Saucy there was no way Sarah was going anywhere. After all, she and John are always falling out over one thing or another. Whatever they say, they never mean it, and they're always really sorry afterwards.

In any case, I wasn't wrong about Sarah moving in with Josie. Of course that's not going to happen. She's just staying for the one night. One night's a whole lot different to every night forever. I'm sure even Saucy can manage one night without her snuggle. If she's that scared of being on her own

in the dark, she can sleep on the rug on the landing with me. You see, that's the sort of kind-hearted dog I am.

If only I knew where she'd got to, I could tell her ...

Saucy:

I'm usually very **careful**. I think about things before I do them. I look at them **calmly** and **sensibly** and then I decide if they're a good idea or not.

But how can a cat be **calm** and **sensible** when her world's about to **change forever?** When she's about to lose the person she loves more than anyone else on the planet? When she's about to have to face **night** after **night** in the **dark** all by herself?

Sometimes being **calm** and **sensible** is too much to ask even of a **coolly careful cat** like me.

Trouble is, now I'm beginning to think I may have done something a little bit **silly.**

Now I'm in the **dark** on my own anyway.

And I've no idea how long before someone finds me.

No idea how long I've got to stay here.

Gruff:

I've been looking. John's been looking. John and Sarah's mum's been looking. Now their dad's got home from work, and he's looking too. We've searched just about every nook and cranny. And it's surprising how many nooks and crannies there are in a house and

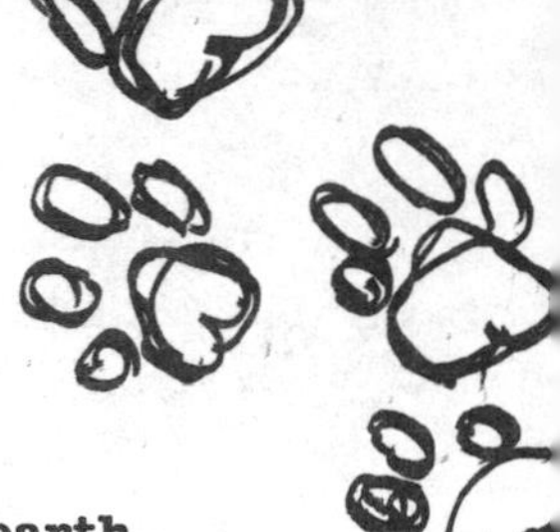

garden when you're hunting for a missing cat.

But there's no sign of her.

Not a trace of a whisker.

Saucy, you daft moggy, where on earth have you got to?

DAY 6

Gruff:

I was up all night. Never slept a wink. I sat by that cat flap, eyes wide open, ears pricked.

She'll come back in a minute, I kept thinking to myself. I may find people hard to work out at times – for instance, how the family can all be in bed happily fast asleep upstairs when Saucy's out there, lost and alone, I will never understand. But Saucy, now there's a cat I can honestly say I know more than a little about.

I know, for example, that her favourite flavours for snacks are tuna and pilchard. I know she hates it if you sneak up on her when she's asleep and go,

'Grr-woof'.

(It's worth it, though, just to see the way her tail shoots up in the air.) I know she sometimes loses count of how many bottom-of-the-stairs grooming sessions she's had in a day, although she'd eat her way through a dog chew rather than admit it.

And I know why she's scared of the dark. But then, if I'd been dumped in the middle of the night, shut up in a cardboard box behind a dustbin at the bus station, like she was when she was a kitten, I'm sure I'd be scared of the dark, too. She didn't know where she was or what was going to happen to her. In the end, someone came across her and handed her in to the rescue centre, which is where Sarah found her.

So, as happy endings go, I've always reckoned that coming to live here was a pretty good one. Saucy's got a great life now. She's loved, cared for, well fed. She gets a seemingly endless supply of cuddles. The family adores her. Which is why I was slightly confused by the fact that they weren't up all night like me, worrying about her, and scratching their heads – or in my case my left ear – wondering where she could have got to.

I mean, how was I to know the panic was over? Was I there when the news came through yesterday evening that Saucy was safe and well and would be back at home in the morning? No. I was where I always go when I need space to think – behind the garden shed. And did anyone bother to tell me when I reappeared in the kitchen that the Great Saucy Disappearing Mystery had been solved?

SCRABBLE

No. They just patted me on the head and sat down to play Scrabble.

People – pah! No matter how much you love them (and I'll be honest, most of the time I'm quite happy to do the whole devoted dog thing), there are moments when I have to ask myself – what are they all about?

Saucy:

We're home. Sarah and me. I sat on her lap in the back seat of the car, peeping out of the window, as her dad drove us back. When I spotted the chip shop on the corner, I knew we were nearly there.

Gruff went mad the minute we were inside the front door. He dashed this way, then that way. He picked up a shoe. He shot halfway up the stairs. Don't get me wrong, it's lovely to be given a welcome, but when he ran through John's legs and knocked him flying into his mum's cactus collection, everyone had to agree that perhaps he'd gone a little bit too far.

'Where have you been?' he panted. **'We've been looking everywhere. I was beginning to think we were never going to see you again.'**

'Didn't you get the message?' I asked.

'What message?' he yelped.

'Sarah rang yesterday from Josie's.'

'But we only discovered you weren't here after she'd gone,' Gruff answered. **'Sarah didn't even know you were missing.'**

I felt a bit sheepish – which, I'll be honest, is an odd feeling for a cat.

Then, 'She did when she found me,' I said.

If Gruff could have sat back and folded his arms, like Sarah's mum does when she's had 'enough nonsense for one day', I think he may well have done so at that moment. Instead, he crouched down on his haunches and narrowed his eyes.

Oh dear. This was going to take quite some explaining.

DAY 7

Saucy:

I never meant to end up in trouble. I certainly don't think of myself as a naughty cat. It's just that I could see Sarah was definitely going somewhere with her toothbrush and that could mean only one thing: wherever she was sleeping that night, it wasn't here.

Her bag was all packed and lying on the bed. I jumped onto her pillow to get a closer look. And that's when I realised. It hadn't been zipped up yet.

I pushed my nose into the opening. I pushed a little more until my head was inside the bag. But I didn't like that. There wasn't much room in there and it was too, too dark, so I pulled it out again quick.

I'm not sure exactly how the idea came to me. I don't remember thinking, that's it, that's what

I'll do! It should have been the last thought I'd have had, given how much a hate squeezing into small spaces – especially small, dark spaces.

I suppose it was just the worry of Sarah going away that made me do it – going who knows where for who knows how long. I didn't know where Josie lived. I guessed it was close by, but it may as well have been on the other side of the world for all the difference that made. Sarah was still going to be fast asleep there tonight instead of fast asleep here. Her pillow on her own bed was still going to be empty. And I'd still have to face a night without her.

So I did it. I snatched a quick look round. There was no one in the room. I took a deep breath, pushed my head into the bag and wriggled the rest of the way in.

I think I was sitting on Sarah's pyjamas, but it was too dark to see. One thing was certain, though. If I stayed on the top she might easily spot me there when she came back to do up the bag. I'd have to bury myself. As if I wasn't squashed enough, I'd have to get squashed even further, but there was nothing for it. If I didn't want to be left alone with Sarah's empty pillow I'd just have to get on with it.

I closed my eyes tight and began to squirm; in amongst the pile of packed things, trying not to disturb them too much; keeping my tail as close around me as I could; nearly to the bottom of the bag.

When I thought I was hidden well enough, I curled up into a ball and half-opened one eye.

It was totally black.

It was hot.

I wasn't even sure I'd have enough air.

And just when I thought I couldn't go through with it and I'd have to get out, Sarah must have come back into the bedroom.

Only a moment later, the bag was zipped shut.

I've done some panicking in my time, but that! It was as if I was a kitten again, right back in that box dumped behind the dustbins at the bus station. I could almost hear the rumble of those late-night coach engines; smell the choking fumes as those huge people-carrying monsters growled in and roared out. I still remember how the stink of them made me feel sick – as if I wasn't feeling sick enough with fear; with wondering what on earth was happening and where I was going to end up.

All right, so this time it shouldn't have felt so bad. This time, I was in a bag belonging to

Sarah. This time, I'd climbed in on my own. It was my choice. This time, I hadn't been dumped, I'd managed to dump myself – in a right old muddle, I must say. But none of that seemed to make any difference, not right there and then. I still felt sick. I was still **terrified**. Sarah was out there somewhere, but so what? I was all alone in that bag.

I was in the dark with no way out.

When I was telling all this to Gruff, he kept shaking his head and going, **'What was the problem? If you didn't like it, all you had to do was make a huge rumpus. I've heard you cats when you start squabbling. You can make more noise than a pack of dogs after a stray sausage. Sarah would have got you out quick as a wink.'**

He's still saying it this morning. **'Why didn't you just make a noise and save me from a sleepless night?'**

I suppose he's right, I should have made a fuss. I should have meowed the minute Sarah zipped up the bag. If that didn't work, I should have yowled my head off when I felt it being lifted off the bed and jolted this way and that as it was carried downstairs. I should have made such a din when I guessed I was being loaded into the boot of the car, and I should have kept on making it until someone realised that I was shut inside, and let me out.

But, somehow I just couldn't. I could hardly breathe let alone get going with all that caterwauling. Not that Gruff will ever understand. Now there's a dog who's never lost for a bark.

I honestly don't know how, but I think I might have fallen asleep in that bag. Perhaps because it was so stuffy. Or maybe the whole horrible experience had just worn me to a

frazzle.

It must have been hours later, hours and hours, when Sarah finally picked it up again. It had been unloaded, I guessed at Josie's, and plonked down who knows where.

I didn't recognise any of the sounds around me. But then, why would I? This wasn't my house. When the doors closed, they made a different sort of click. And the floorboards didn't creak in the same kind of way. Even the sound of footsteps was nothing like at home. I could have been anywhere – in the kitchen or the bedroom; on a chair or under a table.

But when the bag finally moved again, I knew Sarah was there. I could hear her laughing and talking. She was going on about brothers, especially twin brothers, and how grateful Josie should be that she didn't have one.

That's when I heard the zip on the bag being opened. It made a weird, buzzy, grating sort of sound as Sarah yanked it backwards.

'It's not as if brothers do anything useful,' she was saying. 'They're always in the way, they smell funny, and they lose vital pieces of your favourite jigsaw puzzles. If I could choose between having a twin brother and not having a twin brother, I'd –'

And there she stopped short.

She'd been taking things out of her bag as she talked. The weight of clothes pressing down on me was getting less and less, and there was light beginning to trickle through.

Suddenly, a huge shaft of brightness flooded through the opening! It must have lit me up like a Christmas tree.

I gazed upwards and blinked – and there was Sarah's face, gazing back at me. Her mouth was open. I think perhaps mine might have been, too. She looked ... well ... flabbergasted.

Probably so did I.

I've no idea what was going through Sarah's head as she scooped me up, but she gave me the hugest of hugs – the sort of hug people seem to give to someone they haven't seen for a long time. That was odd, obviously, as Sarah had only seen me that morning, but very nice all the same. After all, let's face it, I've had better days.

The relief of being out of that bag and safe in Sarah's arms was like dreaming you were lying on a rubbish tip, then waking up to find yourself on the softest of cushions. I was purring and snuggling. I think I may have been trembling too, because Sarah suddenly grasped me round the tummy, held me in the air, and started to look me carefully all over.

'You funny little cat,' she was saying. 'You're not hurt, are you? You're shaking. How ever did you end up in my bag? Have you been zipped up in there all day? You never even made a sound. **You're so brave!** Braver than I'd ever be. Especially as you're a cat with NITS. Cats with NITS need comfort and cuddles. The last thing they should have to be is shut up in a bag.'

When Sarah went to phone her mum, I had a horrible feeling that that would be it and I'd be dropped off back home. After everything I'd been through, I'd still have to spend the night lonely and snuggleless. But no. Josie's mum said I'd come on such an incredible journey that the least they could do was let me stay.

Sarah was like a cat with two tails – over the moon in other words. Although why people think having two tails would be a happy thing for a cat, I haven't an idea. I have enough trouble keeping my one in order. It's always getting caught somewhere or stepped on. And when the weather's damp, the fur can go so frizzy. You wouldn't believe how many bad tail days I have to put up with. No, believe me, one tail's enough for any cat.

So there was Sarah doing lots of high-pitched squealing like she does when she gets over-excited, and there was me thinking, 'You squeal away'. I admit there are times when that noise of hers can get right on my nerves, but not that night. The cat was out of the bag and back with her Sarah. I was so relieved at that moment, I'd be surprised if anything ever got on my nerves again.

DAY 8

Gruff:

Saucy didn't deserve an adventure like that. I'm the one who needs the adventures. Lots of them. That's the sort of adventurous dog I am.

If I'd been zipped up in a bag, you wouldn't catch me closing my eyes, turning into a big blob of quivery, shivery jelly and wishing it was all over. The only thing I'd have been wishing for was to end up somewhere really, really interesting, like ... a supermarket or a fire station or ... Buckingham Palace! Imagine having that ENORMOUS garden to run around in, not to mention all those huge, long corridors inside. I could spend days just tearing about, exploring, getting lost, then finding myself again! Think of all those new smells. My nose would go crazy! Just the thought of it's giving it a twitch.

It would be more fun if John was with me, of course – although I doubt he'd fit inside a zip-up bag. But if he did, there we'd be, just the two of us – the daring Holly Hill Adventurers. The sort of dog and boy partnership people write books about; make films about; never stop talking about. I'm telling you, I'd be great.

You see, that's the difference between dogs and cats when it comes to adventures: dogs can stand the excitement. Cats, I'm sorry to say, just can't.

Saucy:

Gruff's in a huff. He says it's not fair. I've had an adventure while all he got to do was sit by the cat flap and worry about me all night. He said if I'd made the most of the 'experience' it wouldn't have been so bad, but I didn't – and why couldn't it have been him who got zipped up in a bag instead of me?

Of course, if it *had* been Gruff who'd got zipped up in Sarah's bag instead of me, on the one hand I suppose that would have saved me spending half a day in the dark. But on the other, Sarah wouldn't have had that chat to me. Not then, anyway. She wouldn't have told me that nowhere is too small or too dark or too lonely for God to be there with you. She wouldn't have explained that He'll never say, 'Sorry, but I'm not going there', because He wants to be beside you in even the emptiest, darkest places. Whatever's going on, He wants to share it, stay right there next to you. Oh, you can worry. You can be frightened. You can even think you're all on your own. But you're not! God's always there to take you by the paw (or the hand, of course) and help you through.

I think that somewhere inside me, while I was buried in pyjamas and a towel, a clean T-shirt and that pair of yellow shorts Sarah wears just about everywhere at the moment, I knew all that about

God. Little by little, I suppose I'm finding out quite a lot. Sarah shows Him to me. She's always talking about Him and telling me how He's helped her. She loves praying to Him, she says, and reading the Bible.

'That's how you get to know God,' she tells me. 'You have to spend time with someone if you want to find out about them and know them really well.'

So, although it was a bit scary being lost in Sarah's luggage, I think a part of me guessed I wasn't on my own. God's promised to be with us every day, Sarah says, and He never breaks His promises.

Now what I have to do is try to remember what He's promised when it starts to get dark at the end of each day – and trust God that He'll be there with me, even if Sarah is away for the odd night.

It's not going to be easy to do. Being dumped behind a dustbin's enough to make it hard to trust anyone. But it's either that or I'm going to have to get used to hiding away in zip-up bags, and, if I'm honest, I don't like that idea much.

DAY 9

Gruff:

'Gruff,' said PC Cropper, putting on his policeman's helmet, 'as you know, my faithful dog, George, broke his leg last week in the course of stopping a bank robbery. He'll be all better and back to his crime-fighting best in a few weeks. Meantime, I need a dog I can rely on. How would you fancy stepping in to help me out till he's back on his four feet again?'

How would I fancy it? Does he really need to ask? I'd fancy it as much as I'd fancy lightly grilled bacon on a bed of freshly scrambled eggs for breakfast every morning! By that I mean totally.

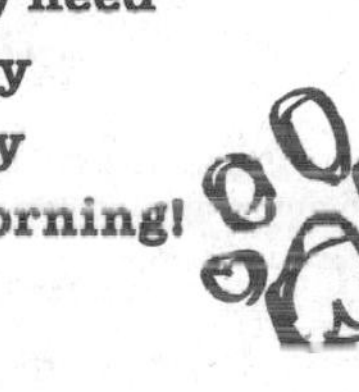

I'm running round and round in circles now, doing a few leaps in the air and yelping excitedly. Do you think PC Cropper's getting the message? YES, PLEASE, I'D LOVE TO STEP IN AND HELP OUT! Look at me, I'm doing that sit up and beg thing that Sarah

always says is so 'cute' ... oops ... I think I might also be dribbling. Not pretty.

So where are we going? What are we doing? What's our first job? Ready for action, that's me. Just say the word, PC Cropper, and I'll be off like a rocket!

'Gruff ... Gruff!'

Yes, yes, I'm here, ready and waiting to obey your every command.

'Gruff, stop kicking me!'

Kicking you? I'm sorry, I didn't realise I was. But as you can feel, I've got very powerful legs – which, I'm sure you'll agree, is a good thing for a police dog. They do seem to have a bit of a mind of their own, but if it's speed you're after, you've come to the right four pins ...

'Gruff, for the last time, WILL YOU WAKE UP!'

What ... ? Noooo, not again! This can't be just another dream.

I opened an eye. Saucy was sitting on the floor, glaring up at me crossly.

'Why?' I moaned. 'Saucy, why do you always have to wake me up just when I'm getting to the good part?'

'The good part?' **Saucy snapped.** 'Oh, and that would be the part where you kick me right off the sofa because you can't keep your legs under control while you're asleep, would it?'

I'm not wrong about cats, you see. They just don't get the whole 'need for adventure' thing. They don't understand that dogs are built for thrills and excitement in the

same way as cats are built to roam around other people's gardens and have ten-a-day grooming sessions. They just don't get that while they're quite happy to lie around in the sunshine all day, dogs want to be out there running in it.

There's nothing for it. As soon as John lets me out in the garden, I'm going to have to go behind the shed.

Saucy:

This is more like it. A whole sofa all to myself. D'you know, when I stretch myself out, I'm actually very long? I need a whole sofa to myself. John says that if I spread myself like this on the floor in front of Sarah's bedroom door, I'd look like a draft excluder. But you won't catch me lying in a draft.

And I'll tell you something else you won't catch me doing: curling up in that damp, weedy, dirty place behind the garden shed. Gruff can keep that as far as I'm concerned. Warm, soft and comfy, that's what I like. And a sofa in the sun without Gruff on it is just about …

((purrrrfect.))

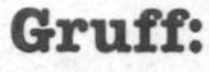

Gruff:

Damp, weedy and dirty, that's what I like. Saucy can have the sofa. It's a bit too warm, soft and comfy for a rufty-tufty adventurer like me. I like to rough-and-tough it out. Get back to my wild dog roots. My ancestors would be dead proud of me, I know they would. If they could see me behind my shed, they would cheer that little wooden hut down.

You see, what no one knows – not even Saucy who, to be fair, probably does know most things there are to know about me – is that my expeditions behind the shed don't begin and end there. All right, so to start with they did. I'd sneak in under the old wheelbarrow, wriggle my way through the

brambles, and then I could pretend to be anything I chose – a wolf stalking through the forest; a bear hungrily roaming the woods. I've even imagined I was a lion prowling about the jungle, though I'd never let on to Saucy.

But that was before I discovered that loose panel in the fence; the fence that separates John and Sarah's garden from next door. That was before I found out that, if I nudged it sideways with my nose, a little gap appeared. And that was before I realised that that little gap was just big enough for a small grey dog like me to slip through and make my way into forbidden territory!

The first time I did it, I was scared witless.

You see, if this was Mrs Allbright's garden, I know I'd be safe as houses. Mrs Allbright is the kind lady who lives on the opposite side of John and Sarah's house to this one. She comes in and childminds from time to time and she loves dogs. I could pop through the fence onto Mrs Allbright's carefully mown lawn, have a rootle around and come back with some trophy or other without even having to break into a run. But, besides the fact that there's no way for a dog to get into her garden from ours, where would be the fun in it?

On the other side, though, live Mr and Mrs Grant.

Mr and Mrs Grant don't keep pets. They won't have them in the house. Not so much as a gerbil, the reason being that Mr Grant has an allergy to animal hair. It sets him off sneezing or itching or coming out in a nasty rash apparently. Something of that sort anyway. So the last thing they're going to want is next door's dog sneaking into their garden ...

Now, there's a challenge if ever I met one. If I can't be a superhero or a police dog or a stunt dog in the circus, I tell myself, at least there's that loose fence panel. When I slip through to Mr and Mrs Grant's garden, the game is on.

What can I find to bring back and bury behind my shed?

And can I get safely in and safely out again with my prize, without being spotted? Because if Mr Grant should see me, I'd be in more trouble than there are dog biscuits in the pet superstore.

I left Saucy stretched out on the sofa. You can sleep the day away if you want, I thought. I've got bigger fish to fry.

John was in the kitchen eating a yoghurt.

'Hey, Gruff,' he said, 'you're just in time,' and he put the empty pot down on the floor for me to lick out ... Mmm ... black cherry. My favourite.

When I'd finished, John picked up the pot and went over to the bin. By the time he turned round, I was already sitting meaningfully by the back door. I'm very good at getting him to open it when I want to go outside. I turn on the whole big-eyed staring

thing like I do when I want feeding. I fix my eyes on the door handle and, just once or twice, glance soulfully back at him over my shoulder. It works a treat every time.

'What is it, Gruff?' said John. 'Do you want to go out?'

Got it in one ... and off I went into the garden.

Today's Great Next Door Garden Challenge was about to begin.

DAY 10

Gruff:

Saucy's not speaking to me. She says whatever it is I get up to behind the shed, I'm not to drag her into it. Never ever.

In actual fact, I didn't drag her into anything. I just sort of ended up landing on her when I'd managed to make my escape.

Well, how was I to know Mr Grant would be round the side of his house up a ladder painting the guttering? Usually he only does things like mowing the grass or cutting the hedge, which isn't a problem. When he's on the ground, he's easy to spot. But standing at the top of a ladder, now that's a completely different story.

I'd squeezed through the gap in the fence like I always do. There's a big bush on the other side, so it's dead easy to skulk behind there and have a good look round to check no one's about before setting a paw out into the open. As far as I could see, there was no sign

of anyone. But the back door was slightly ajar so I knew there must definitely be at least one Grant at home.

This could be exciting, then. I needed to get to the rose bushes over to the right and as the door wasn't shut, that might mean someone was about to step outside at any moment.

Standing on a little circle of gravel near the rose bushes is a stone birdbath. I've never actually seen a bird having a bath in it, but it looks pretty. Around the base of the birdbath is a collection of pebbles. I've seen some like it at the seaside where John and Sarah's parents take us all from time to time. Maybe that's where they come from, I really don't know, but they're round and smooth, and just perfect for me to scoop up in my mouth. The reason I know this is because, on previous trophy-hunting visits, I've managed to carry off one or two. They're now safely buried in my trophy hole behind the shed – along with a spoon, the lid of a sandwich box, an empty can of bicycle oil, two small flowerpots, a piece of knotted string and several old, empty seed packets.

From my hiding place behind the bush, there was one particular pebble that caught my eye. I didn't remember it from before. Perhaps it was a new one. It was slightly

larger than the others and a very pale, soft grey with stripes of a darker grey running all across it. That's the one, I thought instantly, that's today's trophy. Now, how to go about getting hold of it ...

I inched forward through the bush. Nose out first; head, ears. There was definitely no one in sight ... This was it ... go, go GO!

I shot across the grass –

lightning fast

if I do say so myself. I'm convinced I'm part greyhound, although when I mention that to Saucy she just sniffs and replies, 'Part greyhound, part hamster.' All I can say is, she should see me flying through Mr and Mrs Grant's back garden, then she'd laugh on the other side of her whiskers.

The roses were quickly within reach. One leap and I was there, safely tucked in behind them. Ears pricked, I scuttled to the far end of the row of bushes and peered around the corner to the birdbath. There was my trophy, positively glowing in the afternoon sunshine.

And that's when I spotted the tennis ball.

I've no idea why Mr and Mrs Grant had a tennis ball in their garden. They didn't look the type to play tennis and they certainly didn't have children. It was just lying there, looking a bit muddy and out of place in amongst the flowerpots lined up against the side of the house.

I haven't got a trophy tennis ball, I thought. I've got the rubber ball John throws for me when we go to the park but that's different. This would be my very own, extra secret ball to add to my very own, extra secret trophy collection. No contest, then. The pebble could wait until my next expedition. What I wanted now was to get that tennis ball.

It should have been quite easy. I had a clear run between the end of the rose bushes and the flowerpots. It would take a bit of nerve to get up that close to the house but after my earlier police dog dream, I felt I was ready for anything ... I crouched low, tummy to the ground, scooting silently along almost on tiptoe.

My heart was pounding. I hardly dared breathe.

This was the life! This was what I was born for!

I was a daring adventurer about to carry home a priceless, lost treasure!

I was a hero!

I was triumphant!

I was – in so much trouble!

'OI!'

I think I probably spotted Mr Grant only a split second before his angry shout reached my ears. I was midway between the roses and my muddy tennis ball prize. Needless to say, I froze. There he was, round the side

of the house at
the top of a long
ladder, glaring
down at me in
complete disbelief,
paintbrush in hand
– although I have
to say, it didn't
stay in his hand
for long.

For one brief moment, I
saw it poised in his grasp. The
next, it came hurtling through the
air towards me.

I forgot the tennis ball – who wouldn't in that situation? – turned tail, and ran. Not quickly enough, sadly. The brush caught me with a wet smack. It didn't hurt really, but black paint, smeared itself all across my hair down one side.

I didn't stop to inspect the damage. I just continued to hurtle across the lawn. When I reached the bush, I threw myself behind it and dived through the gap in the fence. Only when I was safely the other side did I stop for a second's breather ... but a second was all I took.

'It went behind that bush, Marjorie!' I heard Mr Grant yelling, presumably to Mrs Grant, and the thudding that followed told me they were heading heavy-footedly across the grass after me.

Out from behind the shed I charged,

squeezed under the old wheelbarrow, gave one brief glance over my shoulder and – crashed straight into Saucy. I ran into her with such force that we somersaulted over each other, ending up in John's mum's pansies. This wouldn't have been so bad – I've always known Saucy's tougher than she looks – but, of course, I was covered in black paint ...

Saucy:

All right, that's enough. Gruff's really starting to wind me up now. I've made it perfectly plain that I'm never speaking to him again. Every time he tries to talk to me, I present him with my tail. I mean, what will it take for him to get the message?

'Oh, come on, Saucy,' he keeps saying, **'you have to admit it was all a bit of a laugh. Try and see the funny side.'**

Well, if there's a funny side to what happened yesterday, then I'm a ... duck-billed platypus!

I ask you, what's 'funny' about having a quiet roam out in the garden only to find yourself getting flattened by an annoying little dog and covered in thick, sticky, black paint in the process?

And what's 'funny' about the neighbours hammering loudly on the front door and threatening to have Sarah and John's 'mangy animals taken away if they can't keep them under control'?

And what's 'funny' about Sarah and John's mum assuming that I'm just as much to blame as

Gruff for whatever's gone on because I happen, through no fault of my own, to be covered in the same thick, sticky, black paint as he is?

And what's 'funny' about being picked up by the scruff and dunked up to my neck in a bath full of hot, soapy water to get rid of the paint that shouldn't have been there in the first place, when

I HATE GETTING WET?

I shall be having bad tail days for a month.

So, forgive me, Gruff, if I'm finding it just a little hard to crack a smile at the moment. But not to put too fine a point on it,

CAN YOU BLAME ME?

Which is why I'm heading for the top of Sarah's mum's wardrobe. It's not the most comfortable place to huddle up and get over the whole bath time trauma thing but at least up there Gruff can't reach me to keep sticking his silly black nose in my face.

DAY 11

Gruff:

This is a worry.

Mr Grant's been round huffing and puffing about having to mend the fence. He went on and on.

'It's not my job, you see,' he said. 'I'm not the one with the animals. It should be you keeping them in, not me having to keep them out. So I may have sorted things on my side, but if I were you, I'd get round the back of your shed and make sure not so much as a centipede can get through. Because if I see that scruffy-looking mutt in my garden again, there's going to be more trouble than you'll know what to do with.'

Scruffy-looking mutt? Is he talking about me? Charmed, I'm sure. I'd like to see how good he looks covered in black paint.

But that's not what's worrying me. What's worrying me is that John's mum replied with, 'I'm so sorry, Mr Grant. I guarantee it won't happen again. I'll make sure my husband has a good look at what's going on behind the shed the minute he gets home.'

The minute he gets home? But that can't be very long now. You see, although Mr Grant says he's mended the fence on his side, with

a little bit of jiggery-pokery there's every chance I'll still be able to find a way through. I'm very inventive by nature. But if John's dad has a go at it from this side, too, that'll give me double the trouble.

Only, actually, it's not even that that's really bothering me. The really, really bothersome thing is my trophy hole. My trophy hole behind the shed that's full of my trophies (obviously). The ones I've taken from next door. If John's dad starts digging around, he's bound to find them. I mean, what's he going to think? How's he going to react?

And, more importantly, what's he going to do with them?

DAY 12

Saucy:

I can't believe I agreed to it. I must be going soft.

As soon as Mr Grant had gone back home yesterday, Gruff was pacing up and down, whimpering and even scratching at the back door to be let out into the garden. But John's mum had gone upstairs to make a phone call, John and Sarah were out and about with their Topz mates and it wasn't even time for Gruff's walk, so nothing doing on the being let out front.

I've never seen him acting like that before – not so nervous and agitated. I know I said I was never going to speak to him again, but how was I to know he was about to start behaving as if he hadn't been outside in a month? Call it curiosity if you will (which, by the way, did not kill the cat, it just made him a lot better informed), but I had to know what was going on ... which meant, sadly, that I needed to talk to him.

'Gruff – what?' (I said I needed to talk to him, I didn't say I had to be polite.)

The next thing I knew, he was pouring his heart out about trophies he'd collected and buried in a trophy hole behind the shed and how, if they were discovered, he'd be beside himself because of what he'd gone through to save them and – **'Please, please, pleeeeease, I know it's a lot to ask, but would you mind just nipping through the cat flap and rescuing them for me?'**

I was almost speechless. Almost. But not quite.

'What?' I growled. Oh, yes, cats can growl, too, you know. 'You want me to crawl under the old wheelbarrow and cut myself to pieces on those brambles to get behind the shed, just so I can dig up whatever nonsense it is you've buried there? After the way you covered me in black paint the other day which meant I got dunked in a hot bath, the one thing in life I spend my time purposefully avoiding? I think not!'

'But, it's not hard getting under the wheelbarrow,' Gruff panted, **'and, honestly, if you stay really low to the ground, there's no chance you'll snag yourself on those brambles. And I know you don't really like**

small spaces, but it's actually quite a cool spot behind the shed. I'll share it with you, if you like.' He paused. The tip of his little pink tongue was poking out from in between his teeth. **'I'll do anything you want,'** he begged. **'I'll let you have the sofa all to yourself for the next month ... the next six months ... the next year. I won't go near it. And I promise I won't chase your friends the next time you invite them into the garden.'**

I've heard people say that dogs and cats don't really have expressions. Their faces simply are the way they are. No one could say that about Gruff right at that moment. He had,

'Please help me,

I'll be your friend forever'

written all over him. I was used to him being excitable, annoying, uncontrollable and, now and again, barking mad, but this was none of those. This was ... desperate.

When John and Sarah aren't arguing each other's heads off, they're actually very kind to each other. If one of them has a problem, the other one's right there supporting them and trying to help sort it out. They're like it with the others in the Topz Gang, too, I've noticed. With anyone, probably, truth be told.

They were talking about it one Sunday when they came back from church. Their youth leader, Greg, had been telling them how important it is to be prepared to give each other lots of love and kindness and understanding without expecting anything in return. That's what God wants us to do. It's all a part of being His best friend and showing His love to others. After all, Jesus didn't love people as a way of getting them to love Him back or give Him things He might have wanted. He just loved them for who they were, even if who they were wasn't always the people God wanted them to be. He carried on teaching them and reaching out to them anyway. And He kept on loving them – even when they turned against Him and left Him to die, nailed to a cross so that God could forgive them for all the bad things they'd ever done.

When I looked into Gruff's frantic little face, I suddenly remembered all that and I knew I couldn't turn my back on him. Not because he was promising me this, that and the other (although I suppose it would be nice to be able to have my friends round without them having to watch their backs every second), but because he needed my help. It's what God would want. Simple as that.

'How am I supposed to get these trophies out?' I asked. 'And supposing I manage it, what do I do with them then?'

For a moment Gruff looked totally lost – just like he did as a tiny puppy when John first brought him home. Then –

'No idea, but I'm sure you'll work something out,' he said, and practically bundled me out through the cat flap.

There wasn't much time. John and Sarah's dad could be home at any moment. I'd have to move fast.

When I got to the old wheelbarrow, I stopped and peered underneath. How on earth I was supposed to keep low enough to the ground not to get hooked up on those brambles, I have no idea. And the dirt behind the shed – cobwebs and dust and muck! I mean, what had I let myself in for?

Oh, well, I thought. I'm here now so I may as well get on with it. No time like the present …

And in I went.

It was worse than I ever imagined. I scraped my back on the wheelbarrow; I tore the tip of my ear on the brambles; I got cobwebs all over my face; the soft pink pads on my feet were black with grime, and I broke just about every claw in my toes digging around to find Gruff's trophy hole! Then, to add insult to injury, when I finally uncovered it, what was in there but a dirty pile of old rubbish!

I had half a mind to leave it, but I'd come this far. There was no point not finishing the job. Piece by piece, I pulled, dragged and shuffled Gruff's 'trophies' out from behind the shed. It was no easy task, I can tell you. Dogs may have great big mouths you could carry a football in, but cats are much more dainty. And we're certainly not made to get in a mess. I hardly dared imagine what I must have looked like when I'd finished.

Then, of course, there was the next mountain to climb. Having got all the junk out in the open, I had to find somewhere else to hide it. But where? It wasn't as though ours was the sort of garden that was packed full of suitable trophy holes. Gruff had snuffled out about the only one there was.

There was nothing for it. The whole lot would have to be buried in the bottom of the compost heap. It wasn't ideal, that's for sure. The compost gets dug into and sprinkled on the garden quite regularly, but what was I to do? It was that or nothing. Perhaps Gruff would be able to move it all back to his trophy hole once John and Sarah's dad had finished Gruff-proofing the fence – which I guessed he'd be starting work on any time now.

Just as I'd finished burying that last empty seed packet, home he came.

I dived in behind the compost heap. There was no way I could let anyone see me looking like this. It would mean another dip in a hot bath for sure, and to be perfectly honest, I didn't think my nerves could put up with it for a second time.

No, I'd sit tight behind the compost, carefully hidden between two usefully planted lavender bushes, and clean away every last trace of dirt all by myself. I might wear my tongue out doing it, but I didn't care. By the time I'd finished, I'd be spotless. Even if it took all night …

DAY 13

Gruff:

It feels like ages since John's dad put an end to my 'behind-shed shenanigans' as he's taken to calling my prize-trophy-hunting expeditions. How insulting is that? I mean, what's a 'shenanigan' I'd like to know? Grown-up people love their big words, but if you sat them down and asked them to explain exactly what they mean by them, I bet half of them wouldn't know.

Besides, if there have been any 'shenanigans' going on in this house, it's John's dad who's been getting up to them. He's the one who's moved the old wheelbarrow by the shed onto its side so there's no way to get underneath, and stuck a plank of wood across the gap at the top that's too high to jump over. He's the one who's blocked off my gateway to another world. Now I can't even get in behind the shed to see if he's managed to dog-proof the fence. I've been out there having a look four times now, and it's got me completely stumped.

I know it's only been a couple of days, but I really miss not being able to sneak into Mr and Mrs Grant's garden. I feel all fidgety. I don't know what to do with myself. Not only that, but all my treasured trophies just aren't in a safe enough place any more. The compost heap's no good for hiding anything for long.

Don't get me wrong, Saucy did an incredible job at rescuing them. In fact, I'm seriously having to re-think my whole attitude to cats. No matter how superior they seem, I've always believed they weren't even half as good as dogs.

But I have to admit that what Saucy did for me was **totally awesome.**

All right, so she was gone for hours, far longer than it must have taken her to carry out the trophy rescue. John's dad had got home, completed his 'other-world-blocking shenanigans', had a shower, eaten supper and put his feet up to read the paper for half

an hour before she reappeared.

And talk about a cool cat. Just as Sarah was beginning to think in terms of sending out a search party, in Saucy sauntered, tail held high, looking as though she'd just stepped out of an ultra-posh cat-grooming salon.

She wouldn't say where she'd been or what she'd been up to. She's still barely talking now – just mumbles something about her tongue being red raw, however that happened. But she gave me the wink to let me know she'd done the necessary. By then, I'd already guessed she must have. John's dad certainly didn't seem to have found a thing behind the shed – other than an empty and rather sad-looking trophy hole.

The point is, though, that hole is where my trophies need returning to. That's where they belong. But if I can't even get myself behind the shed any more, how on earth am I going to get anything else there?

Saucy:

I never thought I'd see the day when even two of my ten-a-day grooming sessions would feel like a real chore. Yesterday I barely managed one. But when your tongue feels as though it's on fire from literally hours of heavy grooming, the last thing you feel like doing is treating yourself to another good licking. The only thing I want to do with my tongue just at the moment is stick it in a bowl of ice-cold milk – and leave it there.

DAY 14

Gruff:

It's not easy being a dog. Not when there's something you need to do and you can't work out a way of doing it.

If I was a person, I could take apart that other-world-blocking nonsense (that is to say the plank of wood and the turned-over wheelbarrow) quicker than I could say, 'Woof, there's the postman'. If I was a person, getting back behind the shed wouldn't even appear on the problem scale.

As I'm not a person, but a small dog who can't jump very high, how to hide my trophies safely away in my trophy hole again is actually turning into a major brain-teaser. It's all I can think about.

John took me to the park this morning. As soon as I was off the lead I thought to myself, I'll run my socks off. Not that I generally wear socks, but you know what I mean. Although, having said that, there was that time when I was a puppy and Sarah decided I looked cold. So she dug out the mittens her mum had knitted her when she was a baby and stuck them on my feet. It was a kind thought, but definitely not a good look for a dog.

So anyway, there I was running and running across the grass, backwards and forwards, zig-zagging this way and that. John called me a daft, mad sausage, but I've no idea why. There can't be a sausage on the planet that can move as fast as I can when I put my mind to it. I wasn't even that interested in my ball. All I wanted was to feel the wind whistling through my whiskers and hope it would help me come up with a brilliant plan for getting my trophies safely back where they belonged: behind the shed.

But did it? Did it, doggie chocs.

No, that's not entirely true.

I did have one idea. It's the same one I keep having; the one I come back to over and over again; the one that involves asking a close, furry friend to dig each trophy out of the compost heap where she kindly hid them to avoid discovery, and carry them one by one back to their hidey-hole.

You see, it would be easy for Saucy. She can leap up from the ground to stand on a fence, or sit on a window sill. She'd get over that plank of wood with no problem.

But the trouble is ... I can't bring myself to ask her. She helped me out before, I can't expect her to do it again.

Not only that, but she's bound to start asking questions about where everything came from, and I don't want her to know. She won't understand that my trophies are just bits and pieces it's obvious the Grants don't

want any more. She'll think I've stolen them or something. I know how her mind works.

No, there must be another way. Come on, I'm supposed to be smarter than this. It's a sad day when the only solution to a dog's problem is to ask a cat.

Saucy:

He's at it again. Gruff. Fidgeting about. He can't seem to sit still.

I said to him, 'Gruff, if you don't stop all this pacing around, you're going to wear your legs down. You'll be two inches shorter by the end of the day, and I don't think you can afford to lose that much height, do you?'

He said, **'It may be a joke to you, but if you had a problem to solve, the last thing you'd feel like doing is lying about as if you didn't have a care in the world.'**

I thought, I know I'm going to regret this, but I've got to ask.

'What's your problem this time?' I sighed. 'You're not still bothered about those trophy things, are you? They're a pile of rubbish, Gruff. If someone digs them out of the compost, so much the better. That way they might end up in the bin where they belong.'

'But I don't want them in the bin,' retorted Gruff. **'They're special to me, can't you understand that? Each one of those trophies has real meaning. Each one marks a day when**

I was brave and daring and took off on an exciting adventure into dangerous ...'

He trailed off.

I waited.

Nothing. And Gruff was looking decidedly shifty.

'Into dangerous what?' I asked at last.

He was looking down at the ground as if he knew he'd said too much. Then –

'Territory,' he finished.

I don't always believe Gruff's tales of daring and bravery. He does like to exaggerate when it comes to his expeditions – you know, big himself up a bit, especially when he's been having one of those dreams where he's some kind of superhero.

But this was different. This time he wasn't making things up or showing off. This time he seemed to be trying not to tell me something.

I narrowed my eyes at him. I do that when I don't want any of his nonsense.

'What's going on?' I said. 'You know you'll end up telling me sooner or later, so it may as well be now.'

Gruff flopped down in front of me in a small, hairy heap. He still wasn't looking at me which is always a bad sign.

'It's like this,' he began slowly. **'And please don't take it the wrong way, because it's not how it sounds.'**

I narrowed my eyes further.

'You see,' Gruff went on, **'I'm the kind of dog who needs excitement. I like to do things that are a bit wild and out of the ordinary.**

"Cautious" is not a word that suits me. And while it was fun sneaking into Mr and Mrs Grant's garden, having a nosey round and sneaking out again, what made it extra special was ... the challenges I set myself.'

Challenges? If I narrowed my eyes any further, they'd be shut.

'What challenges?' I asked carefully.

Gruff paused, then, **'Trophy hunting,'** he muttered. **'I'd go into Mr and Mrs Grant's garden, have a scout round, and when I spotted something I liked the look of, I'd bring it back and put it in my trophy hole.'**

I could hardly believe what I was hearing.

'Do you mean to tell me,' I said, 'that everything I took out of your trophy hole and put in the compost heap is stolen? You asked me to help you hide stolen goods?'

'You see?' huffed Gruff, leaping up from the floor. **'I knew that's what you'd think. That's why I didn't want to tell you.'**

'Well, what else am I going to think?' I yowled.

'But it's like you said,' he barked back, **'it was rubbish. Just bits of nonsense the Grants wouldn't miss, let alone want to keep. I was probably doing them a favour getting rid of their litter.'**

No, I wasn't going to listen. There was no way Gruff was arguing his way out of this one.

'Whether they missed them or not isn't the point,' I said quietly. 'You took things from someone else's garden that didn't belong to you. You stole from Mr and Mrs Grant. And you know what that makes you, don't you?' I stood up as tall as I could stretch myself. 'That makes you

a THIEF.'

Gruff:

I feel awful. Saucy's given me a proper telling off, but I can't complain. She's spot-on. Creeping into someone else's garden, a garden where I had no right to be, I suppose that was bad enough. But taking things away from it that didn't belong to me, now that was really terrible.

I've never been called a thief before.

And I feel so ashamed I don't know where to put myself.

DAY 15

Gruff:

For a dog who claims to enjoy his thrills and spills as much as I do, I'm beginning to think I'm actually a bit of a wimp. I've dug a tunnel, scurried backwards and forwards like a demented beetle (all the time trying to make sure neither John nor Sarah nor their mum nor Mr or Mrs Grant sees me), and got myself covered in more dirt in one short morning than I could manage in a lifetime! It should have been a dream come true, but do you

know what? I didn't enjoy any of it.

It was Saucy who made me do it.

When she'd finished telling me off, she said, 'You know what you've got to do, don't you? You've got to put all those trophies back where they came from. Every last one.'

'But how am I supposed to do that?' I yelped. 'I can't get behind the shed any more. And even if I could, between Mr Grant and John's dad and their efforts with a hammer, I can't see there's any way I'll ever be able to get into that garden again.'

Saucy was looking at me with narrowed eyes. She does that I've noticed, but I've no idea why.

'You can dig, can't you?' **she said simply.**

'Er, yes,' I replied.

'Then there's your answer. You can tunnel under the fence.'

I suppose 'tunnelling under the fence' must sound like a fairly simple task to a cat who's never had to dig down further than a few inches to uncover my trophy hole. But what Saucy doesn't seem to realise is that you need space to dig. You need the freedom to get your paws up to speed. That's no easy feat when you're trying to act like an invisible dog at the same time.

To make matters worse, the sky was filled with grey-black clouds. They looked as though they could burst with rain at any moment. I needed to get John to let me stay out in the garden when we got back

from our morning run in the park, but with the weather looking so bad, what were the chances?

Clearly there was only one course of action. I'd have to do what I always do when I don't want to go right back into the house after a walk: pretend I can't hear. It can actually be very effective as a means to get my own way, although I do have to be a bit careful how often I use it. John has been known to threaten to take me to the vet to get my ears cleaned out.

'Gruff!' John called from the back door. 'Come on, it's going to rain in a minute.'

I concentrated on pretending to have a snifty by the gate. I reckon I was pretty convincing, too. I bet John thought I'd found something incredibly interesting.

'Gruff!' he tried again. 'We've got to go in.'

I shuffled forward a few paces and repositioned my nose near the dustbin.

'Gruff, will you please stop snooping about and get in here now!'

It seemed like a good moment to turn my back on him and look as though I was deeply involved in tracking some creature or other along a make-believe trail.

'Fine!' came the shout. 'Stay out here, then. But when it's pouring with rain and you're getting soaked to the skin, don't come whining to me!'

SLAM

went the back door.

That all seemed to go pretty successfully, if I do say so myself.

Now. To work.

I dithered for a moment. Should I fetch the trophies from the compost before I made a start on the tunnel or get the tunnel dug out first? I decided to begin with the toughest job – the tunnel.

The next thing to work out was where to set about digging. The shed was the obvious place. If I could get under the fence as close as possible to the panel that used to be loose, I should just about come out under cover of the bush in the Grants' garden.

The only problem was that the shed was in full view of anyone looking out of Sarah's bedroom or the kitchen window. As Sarah, John and their mum were all at home, the chances of one of them spotting me, scrabbling my way underneath the old wheelbarrow, dirt flying in all directions, were fairly huge. Saucy was on 'distracting duty' (if anyone went near the windows that looked out over the garden, she was instantly to start rubbing up against their legs and meowing for attention), but it was risky nonetheless.

Too risky. I'd have to go under closer to the house.

A cluster of flowerpots stood along the patio edge bordering the lawn. If I kept low to the ground behind them, I could probably dig my way under the fence there without being spotted.

It has to be said that I do have a talent for digging. My paws may only be little but, believe me, they can really shift some dirt. The problem was it wasn't just dirt they had to work their way through this time. There were stones and lumps of concrete under that fence. **Big** lumps of concrete. I scraped and scratched and huffed and panted – but seemed to be getting nowhere incredibly fast. And it wasn't as if I had all day. John might come outside looking for me at any moment.

I was hot and sore and my claws were wearing down to nothing, but I had to keep going. It was important. One of the most important things I'd ever done in my life.

'God's on your side,' **Saucy had said to me before I went out this morning.** 'Sarah says that if we stand up for what's right, God will be right there with us.'

'But I haven't been doing what's right, have I?' I answered. 'I've been stealing. How's God ever going to want to be on my side now?'

'Because you're sorry, Gruff,' **purred Saucy warmly.** 'When we're sorry, God forgives us. And today,' **she added,** 'you're doing the right thing. You're giving back what doesn't belong to you. It might not be easy, but it's God you're doing it for. And it's God who'll make you strong enough.'

Saucy was right, too. I'm sure I'd never have had the willpower (not to mention doggedness) to keep going on my own.

When my nose finally popped out on the other side of the fence in Mr and Mrs Grant's garden, it was the biggest relief of my life. Now all I had to do was make the hole a little larger – enough for me and my trophies – and I'd have done it.

Slowly, I stuck my head out. I needed a quick peep around to check there was no one about. There was no cover here; no bushes, nothing. It was a dangerous place to be.

As far as I could tell, there didn't appear to be anyone in the garden, but I had no way of knowing if I could be seen from the house. The best I could do was scrabble a little more dirt out of the tunnel, then head back to the compost heap for my trophies as fast as I

could. Most of them I'd only be able to carry one at a time, so I'd have to make several journeys. There are moments when I could wish for a bigger mouth. Pelicans don't realise how lucky they are.

I grabbed the empty can of bicycle oil first. As I tore back across the lawn towards my tunnel, at any minute I expected to hear John shouting from the back door – 'Gruff! Drop whatever that is and come inside now.' But Saucy was clearly making an excellent job of 'distracting duty'. Everything was quiet – except for my little heart which was pounding fit to burst.

Just as I dived under the fence, I felt a spot of rain on my nose. No! Not now. Please hold off for a little bit longer.

The empty oil can was one of the first trophies I'd collected. In a way, it was my favourite. Every time I dropped something new into the trophy hole, there it was, looking duller and a bit more worse for rust every day, but it was a prize all the same. I felt quite sad knowing this was the last time I'd ever hold it.

I'd spotted the can on the Grants' grass close to the bush by the loose fence panel. If

I scooted along really fast, I should be able to drop it back there in the exact same spot without any trouble.

Yes! Mission accomplished. Perhaps this would be easier than I thought.

Back in my own garden, I took one of the small flowerpots next. A few more drops of rain had begun to fall. I'd have to move like lightning if I was going to get finished before someone in our house noticed what I was up to.

Quick as a flash I was back wriggling under the fence, pot in mouth.

And that's when I saw them.

Standing on the grass where my tunnel came out.

Two small feet wearing bright red Wellington boots.

I froze.

'Hello, doggy,' said a voice. It was quite high-pitched and, I guessed, a few years younger than John and Sarah's.

The little girl in front of me suddenly crouched down and peered at me.

'What's that in your mouth?'

I was so taken aback, I didn't know whether to stay absolutely still where I was and hope she'd get bored and go away, or turn tail and run. For I moment I even began to wonder if I'd tunnelled into the wrong garden.

But, no. There was the bush I knew, and there were the roses. It was definitely Mr and Mrs Grant who lived here. Only, they didn't have children. They probably didn't even like children. So how come I was suddenly face to face with this one?

'Can I see?' the girl asked.

My mind was whirling. If she wasn't supposed to be there and she was seen (let's face it, those red wellies were very noticeable), there was every chance I'd be spotted, too.

But what if she was supposed to be there? That might not be a good thing either. She might call the Grants over to show them what she'd found under the fence.

All right, now, think, think ... There had to be a way of getting out of this.

The girl spoke again. 'Is that a flowerpot in your mouth? Did you bring it for me?'

Obviously not, but there was no harm in playing along. Carefully, glancing from left to right in case a Grant was about to burst onto the scene, I inched slightly forward and gently put the pot down in front of her. She giggled gleefully, picked it up and ran with it over to a garden bench where she put it down. It wasn't exactly where the pot had come from, but even Saucy couldn't be that fussy. At least now it was on the right side of the fence.

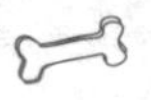

In an instant, the girl was back.

'Do you want to fetch me something else?' she asked.

I looked at her for a moment. I could hardly believe my ears. Whoever she was, and whether she realised it or not, it was possible that this little girl was going to help me return to the Grants' garden everything I'd taken!

No time to waste.

I brought the spoon next. My helper clapped her hands with delight.

'This is a good game,' she cried and ran with it to the bench.

Before long, after a lot of nipping backwards and forwards – me across John and Sarah's lawn and the little girl across the Grants' – there they were, all my trophies lined up side by side – the two small flowerpots, the spoon, the sandwich box lid, the couple of large pebbles, the piece of knotted string and the old, empty seed packets. The empty can of bicycle oil, of course, was out of sight close to the bush.

Done, I thought, and heaved a huge sigh of relief.

All the trophies were back where they belonged.

The trouble was, my helper didn't know that.

'Come on, doggy,' she grinned at me. 'What next?'

What next? There was nothing next, and it was starting to rain that bit heavier now. Any moment, I'd be bound to get the order to go back indoors. I couldn't ignore John again. I didn't want to ignore John again. The thought of curling up, warm and comfy, on the rug on the landing after all my dashing and scrabbling about was just the absolute best.

But how was I going to get away? I didn't want to seem rude. Especially not after my helper had been so ... helpful.

'Jessica!'

The unmistakeable voice of Mrs Grant rang out across the garden. 'Come along in now. It's raining, you're going to get wet.'

'But, Auntie Marjorie,' Jessica called back. 'I want to show you something first.'

What? I wasn't sure what terrified me the most – the fact that Jessica was unknowingly about to give me away to Mrs Grant ... or that Mrs Grant was

actually a small child's auntie!

'Show me later, sweetheart,' was Mrs Grant's response. 'When it's dried up a bit.'

In that moment, Saucy's words from earlier popped into my head. 'If we stand up for what's right, God will be right there with us.'

He was right there with me now, I knew He was. The timing of the bad weather was just about perfect.

It was at the moment when Jessica was saying, 'Bye-bye, doggy. Come back soon so I can show you to Auntie Marjorie,' that I was suddenly aware of another voice.

'Gruff! Gruff!'

It was John.

No! I couldn't go in. Not quite yet. Not until I'd filled in my tunnel. If Jessica took 'Auntie Marjorie' outside the moment the rain stopped, it would be the first thing she'd see. Then there'd be trouble all over again.

I was frantic. John was calling from the back doorway. How much time did I have?

Thinking about it, he probably didn't even have his shoes on yet. In fact he probably didn't even know where they were. He usually didn't. So he wouldn't be likely to step out onto the wet patio straight away. And as long as he stayed where he was, from there he wouldn't be able to see me behind the flowerpots.

Flattening my tummy to the ground, I slithered backwards out of the tunnel. Then as soon as I was back on home territory, I set

to work kicking the dirt furiously back into the hole. I'd dug more of it out than I thought. It was taking too long, and stones kept flying upwards and hitting me on the head. They really hurt! John was going to find me for sure. He'd see what I was doing, he'd guess where I'd been! It would all have been for nothing ... and I'd be in dead trouble.

'Gruff! Where have you got to? Why don't you come inside, you silly dog? Have I really got to come out in the rain?'

By the time John had found his shoes and tracked me down to my spot behind the flowerpots, my tunnel was filled in and the next step of my plan well and truly worked out.

It was simple, really:

LOOK PATHETIC.

Tried and tested, it never failed. And at the moment John found me, looking pathetic was the easiest thing in the world. I was already

wet, cold, bedraggled, exhausted and covered in mud. All I had to add was the droopy ears, big sad eyes and lots of shivering.

'Gruff, what's happened to you? You poor thing!'

John had scooped me up in a second.

'This is all my fault,' he said. 'I shouldn't have left you out here so long. I didn't realise it was raining this hard.'

He glanced down at the trail of dirt around the entrance to my blocked up tunnel. 'What were you doing here? Trying to dig out some sort of shelter for yourself? Oh, I didn't mean it when I said you couldn't come whining to me when you were getting wet. You should have just scratched at the door. I'd have let you in. I've only been playing with Saucy. She wouldn't leave me alone. I'm SO sorry.'

In seconds, we were indoors in the warm. I felt a bit bad making John feel so guilty. But with Jessica's help (not to mention God's), at least I'd been able to do the right thing.

And unlike Saucy,

I LOVE hot, soapy baths.

I was going to wallow in the one John had just run for me for as long as he'd let me.

DAY 16

Saucy:

Much as I don't like admitting it, I'm beginning to realise that there's more to Gruff than I would ever have thought possible. I don't tend to think of him as wise. More ... well ... barmy. And it's hard to put wise and barmy together somehow. Perhaps it's a dog thing. Gruff probably has problems understanding that you can be clever and cuddly, which is obviously a cat thing.

Gruff said, **'Do you know what? All that trophy business has got me thinking.'**

'Really?' I said. 'About what?'

'About the fact,' said Gruff, **'that you and me, we're not actually so different.'**

I happened to be munching on a tuna-flavoured snack at the time. I almost choked.

'Oh, excuse me, but I think you'll find we are,' I spluttered, when I'd recovered myself. 'For instance, do I enjoy getting dirty? Do I need walking every day? Do I smell funny when I'm wet (or when I'm not wet, come to that), or do that ridiculous sit-up-and-beg routine? Do I scratch myself in the most undignified places? I think not.'

'No, I'm not talking about stuff like that,' replied Gruff. **'And by the way, I'm proud of the way I smell. No, I'm talking about how we are and what we need.'**

'And what would that be?' I said, not that I was at all interested. This was obviously just another bit of Gruff nonsense.

But when he began talking, I realised it wasn't nonsense at all. In fact it was the most sense I'd ever known to come out of his mouth.

Gruff said he'd once heard John talking about something called the Holy Spirit. John had been saying that, when someone made friends with God by asking Him to forgive them for all the things they'd done wrong and to take control of their lives, God would give the Holy Spirit to His new friend as a present; a helper to lend a hand with living God's way.

'I didn't really understand what John meant at the time,' Gruff went on. **'But I think that now I do. God wants everyone to live lives that please Him by doing good things instead of bad – not because He wants to spoil**

people's fun and make them miserable, John says, but because He wants them to have the best lives they possibly can. Living God's way means you can do that, because it's God who knows what's good for people and what isn't; God knows what will hurt them, and what will make them happy.

'The trouble is, living life God's way isn't always easy. There are times when it can be really hard; times when it seems easier to do what you want to do, or what other people want you to do, than to do what's right and what God says is good.

'That's where the Holy Spirit comes in. That's why God promised to send His Holy Spirit into the lives of everyone who becomes His friend. The Holy Spirit is there to help people. They can talk to Him, just like they talk to God, and ask Him to help them whenever they find it hard doing the right thing. They can ask the Holy Spirit to help them live the sort of lives that God wants them to live.'

Sitting there, tuna-flavoured snacks well and truly forgotten I might add, it was almost impossible to believe this was Gruff I was listening to. For once in my life, I didn't dare interrupt. Somehow, I didn't want him to stop talking.

'The other thing I've heard John say,' Gruff continued, **'is that sometimes it can be hard for people to face up to the fact that they do wrong things – and even harder to stop themselves doing them. They can try to pretend that everything's all right – just like I did with stealing – but it just isn't. What they need is to let Jesus show them anything they might be doing that's wrong, and then ask the Holy Spirit to help them stop. John says he wants to live God's way, to learn to be more like Jesus, so he asks the Holy Spirit to be with him and to help him every day.'**

Gruff stopped for a moment and looked at me. I think he was quite surprised to find me still awake. I have been known to drop off to sleep before when he's been droning on.

'Now,' he said, **'this is where I think we're the same, Saucy. You see, deep down, I knew it was wrong to go next door and take those things from the garden. But somehow I enjoyed it. It was fun and I wanted the excitement. It was something I thought I needed. Only now Jesus has shown me that it's not right. Taking things that don't belong to me isn't what God wants me to do. So, from now on, whenever I feel like "trophy hunting", I'm going to do what John does. I'm going to ask the Holy Spirit to help me be strong enough to say, "No, I'm not doing that. I'm living God's way."'**

I was staring at him, I know I was. I was gazing at him **with admiration.**

It was a very odd sensation. That's not usually the way cats look at dogs. But then I suppose dogs aren't usually so ... wise.

There was just one thing I didn't understand. How did all of this mean that Gruff and I weren't so different?

'There's something you do, too, Saucy,' said Gruff when I asked him. **'Something you feel that gets in the way of you living the amazing life God wants you to have.'**

'And what would that be?'

'Fear,' replied Gruff. **'You're scared of being all alone in the dark; scared of being left on your own because someone left you by yourself in a box at the bus station when you were a kitten. And no matter how much Sarah loves you or how much she lets you snuggle into her pillow all night, you're still afraid of being dumped again. That's why you hid in Sarah's bag the other night. Because you couldn't bear to be left behind.**

'You and me, what we need is exactly the same. Just as I need to ask the Holy Spirit to make me strong enough not to start stealing things again, you need to ask the Holy Spirit to be there every day to help you be strong and get over your fear. God will never leave you –

you told me that. Now what you have to do is get the Holy Spirit to help you really believe it. After all, it's God's promise to everyone. Then maybe you can start to live your life without being scared.'

DAY 17

Saucy:

When I hear Sarah chatting about prayer, I always think she means talking to God or to His Son, Jesus. I never think about praying to the Holy Spirit – asking the Spirit of God to make you strong so that you can try to get the better of unhelpful feelings like fear, or learn to say no when you think you might be going to do the wrong thing.

I know God knows and understands everyone – better than we know and understand ourselves, I shouldn't wonder, because He made us. I've heard Sarah talking about it lots of times.

But now Gruff's made me realise something else. Although God wants us to follow Him and live His way, He knows that it's hard for us. He understands that we can find doing the right thing all the time a little bit of a struggle. And that's why, when we become His friends, He gives us a present of the Holy Spirit to live in us every day.

Just think: that's the gift of God's power in our lives to help make us strong enough to live for Him.

And do you know what that is?

Wonderful.

DAY 18

Gruff:

Why is Saucy doing that? The last couple of days she's been nice as pie – giving me plenty of space on the sofa; asking how my walks went; even putting up with my fidgety leg problem when I'm dreaming, which normally gets right on her nerves.

Then, this morning, she won't stop looking at me. And I don't mean in a nice way. She's doing the narrowed eyes thing. All the time.

If I lie down for a quick nap, the moment I wake up, she's watching me. If I sit on a chair for a gaze out of the front window, the second I turn round, she's watching me. If I pop out to the kitchen for a slurp from my water bowl, she's glued to me like a slug to a lettuce leaf. If I'm out in the garden playing at being a mountain rescue dog, there she is, head sticking out of the cat flap, never letting me out of her sight.

I've said to her, 'Saucy, what is your problem?'.

But the only response I get is, 'If anyone's got a problem round here, I don't think it's me, do you?'.

It's like I've always said – Cats? We need them like we need a family of fleas setting up house in our hair.

Saucy:

I can't understand it. I'm shocked and I'm disappointed. After everything Gruff said, all his amazing talk about how we should both ask the Holy Spirit to help us live how God wants us to live. How we should use God's gift of power to make us strong enough to say no to doing the wrong thing.

And now this!

Gruff's still stealing. He's still taking what doesn't belong to him.

And this time, it's almost worse than before. This time, Gruff's stealing from ME.

DAY 19

Gruff:

Saucy's still watching me. Accusing me of something or other with her eyes when I don't even know what it is I'm supposed to have done. Glaring at me but saying nothing.

Actually, that's not completely true. She did mutter something to me this morning.

I said to her, 'Have you still got nothing to say to me? Anything would be nice. Just one, little word.'

'One little word?' **she answered.** 'Right, I'll give you one little word:

BISCUITS.'

Sad to say, but Saucy's forced me into having a re-think on cats and fleas. If this is how it's going to be from now on, I reckon I'd rather invite in the flea family.

DAY 20

Saucy:

What can I say? Even cats have to be allowed to make the odd mistake now and again. It doesn't happen much. Hardly at all really and not nearly as often as dogs get things wrong, it's a known fact – at least, it's a known fact in the cat world, although I'm sure dogs would have something different to say about it. And, generally speaking, who listens to dogs?

That said, when I see Gruff when he gets back from his walk, I'm going to have to tell him I'm sorry.

It wasn't my fault, though. I mean, what was I supposed to think?

You see, I came in a bit late the other night. The girls and I had been doing a spot of fence-running. It had gone rather well, actually, and I was ahead of my friend, Sukie, on points, which doesn't often happen. I was just about to get off home for a snack then bed, when Star, the kitten, decided to take a flying leap into an apple tree.

'What are you up to now, Star?' demanded Sukie, flicking her tail crossly. 'Get down, we all want to go home.'

But getting down was the problem. Star's a brave little madam when it comes to climbing up something, but a bit of a quivering wimp when it's time to make her way down again.

'I can't,' Star meowed. It was pitiful really. 'I'm too high up. I'm very sorry about this, but I think I might be stuck.'

'When will you ever learn?' sighed Sukie.

'But that's what kittens do, isn't it?' grinned Madge, the oldest of us fence-runners. 'They get into trouble. I know I did.'

'Well, thankfully I didn't have to climb up apple trees rescuing you,' retorted Sukie.

The next moment, she'd leapt up into the tree and landed neatly on the branch just below Star.

'Right,' she said. 'You needn't think I'm going to do this every time you get yourself in a muddle. But for now, just follow me and do what I do.'

Carefully and gracefully, Sukie sprang down from branch to branch, Star copying her every move (if a lot more clumsily), until the two of them were once more safely sitting on the fence.

I ended up being out that night much later than I'd meant to be. When I finally got home, I was starving. I always like a little something before bed and tend to leave a few snacks in my bowl especially to have a munch on. They were pilchard flavour that day and I was really looking forward to them.

So, imagine how I felt when I got to my dish to find it **EMPTY.**

Not a biscuit in sight. Not a crumb even! Someone had eaten the lot. I mean, I ask you!

Well, it wasn't likely to be Sarah or John, was it? And it certainly wouldn't be their mum and dad. For some reason, they don't even like the smell.

So who did that leave?

Let me see.

Ah, yes …

Gruff.

It's not as if it happened just the once. The last couple of nights, it's been the same thing. I've been keeping an eye on Gruff as much as I can but at some point after dark, I've been going to my dish to find every last snack has been taken.

Again.

Gobbled up.

Munched away by a muncher who has no business to be munching from my bowl!

I didn't want to have to say anything to him. I wanted Gruff to have a think about what he was doing, realise it wasn't right and come and say sorry. All the more so because only a short while ago, he was telling me he was going to ask the Holy Spirit to help him stop stealing. He can't have forgotten already, I thought. He was the one who was talking about it. And all this watching him and waiting – well, to be perfectly honest, it's wearing me out.

So today I decided I'd give myself a break. If Gruff's out for a walk with John, I thought, he can't be stealing my biscuits. I'm popping out for some girl chat.

I found Sukie relaxing on a car bonnet in the road outside her house.

'May I come up?' I asked. It's always best to ask with Sukie. She can get very protective of her space on car bonnets, especially if the car's only just been parked and the warmth from the engine makes it a snug place to lie.

'Of course you can,' Sukie replied. 'It was lovely up here half an hour ago, but it's gone a bit cold now.'

I was just settling myself down next to her when she said it.

'Do you know, it's the oddest thing, but I'm absolutely certain my food's being pinched.'

I think my mouth might have dropped open. Ever so slightly. It was all right though because I had very clean teeth.

'Do you know what's even odder?' I said. 'The same thing's been happening to mine.'

The car bonnet shook slightly as Madge landed beside me.

'I happened to be passing and couldn't help overhearing,' she said. 'So your food's been disappearing, too. I have to say, that's such a relief. I keep going back to _my_ bowl and finding it empty, when I'm sure there was the odd snack left in it. I know I'm getting forgetful in my old age, but I was beginning to think I was losing my memory altogether.'

That was it. That was the moment I realised what a huge mistake I'd made. It wasn't Gruff who'd been stealing my food at all. It couldn't be. One thing he definitely wasn't doing was sneaking in and out of other people's houses at all hours of the night. Gruff can't use a cat flap. It's not that he's too big, he just hasn't got the knack. The only time he ever tried mine, he got stuck.

No. If most of the cat food in the street was disappearing, there had to be another explanation.

The question was, what was it?

DAY 21

Gruff:

I still can't believe it. I can't believe Saucy thought I was stealing her food.

'I'm sorry,' **she said.** 'But look at it from my point of view. Who else could it have been?'

'If you thought it was me,' I retorted, 'you should have just asked me. Instead of which, you've been prowling around after me giving me the heebie-jeebies.'

'I know, and I was wrong,' **Saucy said.** 'Forgive me? Please?'

She was looking at me with huge, soft eyes, and letting the tips of her ears curl ever so slightly down. It was one of her carefully crafted 'winsome' expressions. There's not a person in the world would have been able to

resist it, so what chance did I have?

Of course I forgave her. But that doesn't mean I understand her. Still, that's cats for you. One of the biggest mysteries on the planet. (Gooseberries being the other one, obviously.)

'So anyway,' **Saucy went on,** 'all of that means there must be a thief on the loose. And it's up to us to catch them.'

'Right,' I barked. That sounded as though it could be quite interesting. 'And how are we going to do that?'

'How do you fancy,' **Saucy began,** 'playing secret agents?'

Sometimes, my tail can start wagging when I'm least expecting it. It seems to have a mind of its own. All of a sudden, as I listened to Saucy, that little grey stub of mine began twitching backwards and forwards madly and there wasn't a thing I could do about it. Although this time, I think it was the words 'secret' and 'agents' that probably had a lot to do with it.

A shiver of excitement was tingling along my spine, and, I'm not sure, but I think my mouth might have been forming itself into a huge grin. This was the best thing to have happened since I dreamt I was the President of America's personal bodyguard at his home in The White House.

'If you're after someone to play secret agents with,' I barked as deeply and throatily as I could, while puffing out my chest in what

I hoped was an awesomely secret agenty sort of way, 'you've come to the right dog. What's the plan?'

And if you had to play secret agents with a group of cats, I've got to admit that Saucy and her lady friends would be the right ones to choose. They had it all worked out. When night fell, the job of thief-catching would begin.

Saucy and Sukie were to lie in wait near Sukie's cat flap. Star and Madge would lie in wait near Madge's. (Star said there was no point guarding her own cat flap. She was always so hungry from all her zany chasing about, that she never left any food in her bowl for an intruder to munch on.) If the thief turned up, they'd be ready.

That, of course, left me. My job was to wait in the shadows by Saucy's cat flap inside the kitchen. If anything came in, I had to start barking my head off. Saucy said they'd all hear me and come pelting back. In any case, if I started making that much of a rumpus, I'd wake the family and they'd be downstairs like a shot.

I have to admit that just barking sounded a bit dull. I wouldn't tell the girls, but I had my own plan in mind. This was my chance to prove myself; to show the world it wasn't just in my dreams that I could be a hero.

Now all I had to do was wait for nightfall ...

Saucy:
It's getting late. Sarah and John have gone to bed already.

I hung around in Sarah's room for a little while. She was sitting with her legs stretched out, reading a book – 101 Dalmatians. I've never understood why that story's so popular. If it was 101 Ginger Toms or 101 Tabbies, now that would be so much more interesting.

I lay under Sarah's feet and let her tickle my tummy with her toes. If I'm honest, by the time her mum came in to say goodnight, I didn't feel like moving at all – partly because I was so comfortable, and partly because … well, it could be anything out there stealing cat food, couldn't it?

I mean, supposing it's some wild creature that's escaped from the zoo? Or, worse, some kind of monster? All right, so it would have to be a pretty small sort of monster to get through a cat flap, but small or not, a monster's still a monster … perhaps with long, yellow teeth and sharp, pointed claws and staring, bloodshot eyes …

I tell you what, it's one thing being all brave in broad daylight when you're working up a plan to catch a thief. It's another altogether when the time comes and you've actually got to carry it out … in the dark of the night …

DAY 22

Gruff:

I think it's getting light. It must be nearly morning.

I've been crouched in the shadows, waiting, for hours. My back left foot's gone to sleep and I've got cramp in my right shoulder. As for my nose, it's itching like crazy and I'm desperate for a scratch.

But I daren't move.

I can't give myself away.

It must be ages since Saucy slipped silently out through the cat flap. We exchanged a look before she went. I could see she was frightened. I have to admit to feeling a twinge of fear myself. But at least I had an excuse. After all, Saucy was doing her secret agent bit with a partner. I was having to do mine all by myself.

I wasn't going to let on, though. As far as Saucy was concerned, what I wanted her to see was Gruff the brave. Gruff the plucky. Gruff the most heroic superhero of all time.

So that's what I showed her. The trembling knees and thumping heart I kept to myself ...

What was that?

I heard something.

In the stillness of the night it was unmistakable.

Was it the rattle of the garden gate?

I think possibly so.

That can mean only one thing.

This is it.

This is my moment of glory.

No thief's going to get away with stealing anything from this house while I'm on guard.

I can feel my muscles tensing ... I'm all ready to spring.

That's my plan, you see, to jump out onto whatever it is and sit on it! I might do a spot of growling but forget the barking nonsense. I can do what I've got to do without waking up the whole house, no problem. Leave it to the guard dog to sort out.

Another noise.

There's definitely something out there.

It's getting closer.

I can see the cat flap moving ... opening a little at a time ...

No going back now.

I only hope my knees hold out.

Ready ...

A flying leap and –

GOTCHA!!

Saucy:

The day I plan anything with a dog ever again is the day I start going to puppy training classes.

What a fiasco!

One minute I was making my way as quietly as I could through my cat flap, whispering, 'Gruff, are

you there? It's me.' The next, I was flying through the air as if I'd been shot out of a cannon, to land with a crash face down in the top basket of the vegetable rack. I don't like the smell of onions at the best of times, but this was ridiculous.

To make matters worse, the next minute Gruff's little, round, grey body came hurtling out of the shadows, smacked down on top of me, and the entire rack collapsed. Talk about vegetable mayhem! Onions, carrots, potatoes, courgettes, broccoli and a cauliflower – the whole lot went rolling across the floor, booming like a clap of thunder.

The lights in the hall went on in seconds.

Then came the feet on the stairs. All eight of them.

'What's happening down there?' yelled John and Sarah's dad.

'What on earth's all that racket?' screeched John and Sarah's mum.

'Is it a burglar?' squealed Sarah.

'Is it aliens?' shrieked John.

'No!' I wanted to yowl at him. 'It's a pile of

vegetables, every one of them with more brains than your daft dog!'

I didn't, of course, because I'm a cat. John wouldn't have understood a word.

I'm not sure quite what the family made of it when they stood looking at the mess on the kitchen floor. I think perhaps they thought the rack had collapsed on its own, but I'm only guessing.

'Perhaps the cauliflower was the straw that broke the camel's back, so to speak,' John and Sarah's dad was saying to John and Sarah's mum. I've no idea why as there wasn't a camel in sight, but if he wanted to blame the whole thing on an invisible hump-backed animal, who was I to argue?

Sarah looked very worried and whisked me up in her arms crying, 'Oh, Saucy, you're not hurt, are you?'

John was patting Gruff, not seeming to notice the hairy, little mongrel was wearing his guilty face.

'Of course she's not hurt,' he said. 'It's just some vegetables, it's not the Loch Ness Monster.'

'I'm sure being hit on the head by a cauliflower can be just as dangerous as being attacked by the Loch Ness Monster, if you really want to know,' Sarah retorted.

'Not now,' sighed their mum, on her hands and knees gathering up potatoes. 'It's far too early to start arguing.'

She was right about it being early.

She was so wrong about the arguing.

As soon as we were on our own, the cat and dog fight started.

'What were you thinking of?' I snapped.

'I was thinking of catching a thief,' Gruff growled back. **'What do you think I was thinking of?'**

'But you didn't catch a thief, did you? You caught me!'

'Well, how was I supposed to know it was you?'

'Because I told you as I came through the cat flap!'

'No, you didn't.'

'Yes, I did.'

'No, you didn't.'

'Yes, I did.'

'NO, YOU DIDN'T!'

'YES, I DID!'

'QUIET DOWN THERE!!'

John and Sarah's mum could shout far louder than the pair of us, it seemed. She'd clearly had enough nonsense for one night.

And so had I.

DAY 23

Gruff:

I was almost beginning to think that being a secret agent wasn't all it was cracked up to be. Just a lot of lying around in the pitch black, and ending up sprawled in a heap of vegetables. That's not exactly the heroic end to my thief-

catching that I'd had in mind.

But that was on the first night of my secret agenting.

On the second, it was another story altogether.

'If you see the cat flap move,' Saucy had said when she left that evening to take up her position outside Sukie's house, 'listen before you do anything stupid in case it's me.'

I really didn't like that. I don't do 'stupid'. Excitable, crazy and even zany, possibly. But never stupid.

I'd show that stupid cat, I thought.

Later, when the family was in bed and I was alone in the kitchen, I made myself at home in my dark corner by the cat flap ... and waited.

Perhaps it was a waste of time.

Perhaps it would be like last night and no one would come.

It was deathly quiet.

Not even a car drove by and there wasn't a breath of wind.

I'd hear anyone or anything that came near the house for sure ...

If only my eyelids didn't feel so heavy.

I suppose I could just have one, tiny yawn and maybe stretch myself a little. And I'm sure it wouldn't hurt to make myself the teensiest bit more comfortable. After all, it was hard work last night. It's no wonder I'm sleepy.

Perhaps I could just close my eyes for

a moment ...

It's not as if I'm not wide awake ... I've got my ears pricked and everything ...

SNAP!

I woke with a start.

The kitchen was pitch black. I couldn't see a thing.

But I knew what that snap meant.

It meant the cat flap had just clicked shut. And if it had clicked shut, then some time in the last few moments ... it must have flipped open.

I held my breath.

I daren't move a whisker.

As I strained my eyes to see through the thick darkness, I could just make out some sort of dim shape. It stood, stone still, inside the back door.

My body went rigid and the hair all along my spine stood bolt upright.

I was no longer alone ...

Saucy:

I've never stayed outside very late before now, but I think perhaps I could get used to this being out all night lark. It's so peaceful. And I like watching the moon. Sometimes a cloud covers its face, then slides away and there it is, beaming down brightly again. God made the night sky so beautiful.

I miss Sarah's pillow, and Sarah obviously, but with the help of the Holy Spirit I'm sure I'm a little less scared of being alone in the dark than I was. Gruff may be clueless when it comes to being a secret agent, but he was right about that.

Strictly speaking, I haven't been completely on my own, of course. I've had Sukie with me and she's very good company. But every now and again I've slipped away by myself to find Madge and Star and see how their thief-watch is going, and the shadows haven't frightened me once. In fact, I rather like them.

'Do you know, Saucy, I think we're going to have to give this up,' said Madge. 'I reckon whatever it was that's been stealing our food knows we're here waiting. It's not going to try anything if there's a chance it might be set on by four yowling cats. I know I wouldn't.'

'We can't give up yet,' meowed Star. 'It's bound to come back soon. Perhaps it's just not hungry at the moment.'

'Maybe it isn't,' Madge replied, 'but I certainly am. It's way past my midnight feast time. I'm going in. I'll see you tomorrow.'

'Spoilsport,' Star muttered under her breath, as Madge disappeared through her cat flap.

'No, I think she's right,'

I said. 'That's enough thief-watching for one night. Let's get off to bed.'

Star wrinkled her nose. 'Do you know what I'm not going to be when I grow up?' she said.

'No, what?' I answered.

'Boring,' she replied.

Gruff:

The shape by the back door didn't move; didn't make a sound.

What was it?

As my eyes slowly began to get used to the darkness in the kitchen, the outline became a tiny bit clearer. But only a tiny bit.

I could definitely make out four legs, but what was on top of them was no more than a sort of blob. I couldn't even be sure it had a head. Not from where I was lying.

What was it going to do? Just stand there? What was it waiting for?

Saucy's bowl lay on the other side of the kitchen next to the fridge. There were snacks inside ready and waiting. Whatever the intruder was would have to tiptoe across in front of me to reach them. Would that be the moment to spring out, knock it off its four legs and sit heroically on top of it, trapping it on the floor until help arrived?

Or should I wait until it had its back to me with its head (if it had one) in Saucy's bowl? Perhaps that would have more of the element of surprise.

The trouble was that, crouched in the

darkness, all on my own in the kitchen with some unknown creature, suddenly I was terrified. Scared stiff. I was beginning to wonder if I'd be able to move even if I wanted to.

This wasn't like one of my dreams. In my dreams, being bold and brave was easy. In my dreams, being a hero – well, there was nothing to it.

But this was different.

This was real life.

And it was all I could do not to burst into a whimper.

Why didn't it move?

Why was it just standing there?

If it was trying to freak me out, it was doing a perfect job.

Just do something, why don't you, or are you planning on staying there the rest of the night?

And that's when it did do something. Right there and then.

It started to turn around.

Very slowly.

But not towards Saucy's bowl. Not even back towards the cat flap to slip away to where it came from.

No! The intruder was turning towards ME.

If I could have shrunk any further back into the shadows, I would have done. But my tail was already jammed up against the wall. There was nowhere for me to go.

I was trapped! Cornered in my own kitchen in my own house!

I was right. This was nothing like one of my dreams. This was a nightmare. I never wanted to be a hero **EVER** again!

'Are you going to jump out on me or can we talk about this?'

The voice came out of nowhere. Well, not nowhere exactly. It came from the intruder.

Facing me as it now was, I could see its shape more clearly. It had quite a shaggy body, but even in the darkness, I could see that the fur was sort of lumpy, matted, and not at all well looked-after. The outline of the tail was thin and appeared a little crooked.

Then there was the head. Yes, I could see now that it did have a head.

And I could also see what the head belonged to.

This wasn't any sort of monster. Not even a mini one.

As the creature took a couple of steps closer, I could see clearly that this was nothing more than a mangy-looking ... cat ...

To say I was embarrassed would be putting it mildly. Since when did dogs hide away in the shadows because they were terrified of cats? Since when were dogs terrified of anything? Especially rufty-tufty, daring adventure scouts like me? I'm not sure, but I think this might have been one of the most shameful moments of my life.

'How ...?' I began. 'How did you know I was there? It's pitch black in here.'

'Is it?' replied the cat. He had a much deeper voice than I was expecting. 'I suppose it is, I hadn't really noticed. I've got very sharp eyes, you see. Most cats have. There's not much gets past us.'

'Obviously,' I said, trying to sound as tough as a dog with the name Gruff should sound.

'So,' said the cat, 'were you scared of me just then?'

'No!' I snapped.

'You looked scared,' he shrugged.

'Well, I wasn't, all right? I'm the dog, you're the cat. What's to be scared of?'

'That's what I was wondering. Don't you want to know why I'm here?'

'I know exactly why you're here,' I answered, feeling more confident now. If I handled this right, I reckoned I could still come out of the situation not looking like too much of a poodle.

I stood up and took a couple of steps towards the intruder.

'You're a thief. That's why you're here,' I growled. 'And I'm here to stop you.'

'So stop me,' said the cat – and sat down.

There was something very wrong with the way this was all going. Either this cat had nerves of solid steel or I was losing my touch. Most of Saucy's friends would have scarpered by now. They certainly wouldn't be sitting there, practically nose to nose with me, as if I was nothing more than a small, grey, hairy cushion.

Perhaps it's some sort of trick, I thought, and decided to play the thief at his own game.

I sat down, too.

The cat was looking right at me.

'I'm getting very hungry,' he said after a moment. 'Now I know there are some delicious, pilchard-flavoured snacks in that bowl. I can smell them from here. You don't seem very sure what to do, so, if it's all the same to you, while you're making up your mind, I'm just going to go over and tuck into a few.'

I could hardly believe my ears. The cheek of it! I was on my feet again in no time.

'Do you think this is some sort of joke?' I barked. Quietly, though. I didn't want to wake the whole house up. 'If you think I'm going to let you stroll over and steal Saucy's food, just like that, you've got another think coming.'

'So, chase me,' sighed the cat disinterestedly. 'I'm really not that bothered.'

'Well, you should be!' I retorted. I could feel my hackles rising now.

'It's like this,' said the cat. 'I've been roaming for about six months now. I'm what they call a "stray". I'm never quite sure why I get called that, though. I always thought being a "stray" meant you'd "strayed" away from your own home and needed to get back there.' He paused thoughtfully. 'But I haven't got a home. Not any more. They moved away, you see, my family, and in all the hustle and bustle, somehow I think they must have forgotten to take me with them. One day I went back after a night on the prowl and they were gone. I hung around for a while in case they came back. But they never did. After some time, some new people moved into the house. Almost the first thing they did was have the cat flap blocked up. The last thing they seemed to want was someone else's leftover moggy.

'I've had to become a bit of a chancer, you see,' he finished, giving himself a stretch and flicking his crooked tail, 'sniffing out food where I can whenever I can. When I get found out, I just move on. So, if you want to chase me off, then you'd better get on with it. It doesn't bother me any more. I've been chased off more times than there are hairs left on my tail.'

I was stunned. Speechless.

Never in my life before had a cat made me lost for words. Although, to be fair, apart from Saucy, cats never usually hang around long enough to have a conversation. This was terrible. Here was a cat who'd been abandoned just like Saucy had been abandoned in a cardboard box at the bus station. They'd pretty much been through the same thing.

Except that for this shaggy wanderer, there'd been no happy ending.

DAY 24

Saucy:

I've had some shocks in my time, but this! Climbing in through the cat flap after a hard night of secret agent business to find Gruff and a cat who's seen better days sitting around my empty bowl, chatting away as if they'd known each other for years – well, it was almost enough to knock me off my feet.

'What's all this?' I said.

I wasn't happy. Not only was there no food left in my dish, and I was starving, but there was a strange cat sitting in my kitchen, on my territory, and Gruff didn't seem to be doing a thing about it.

'Well?' I hissed, looking the intruder right in the eye. My back was curving up in an arch. I wasn't in the mood for nonsense. 'I'm waiting.'

'It's all right, Saucy,' said Gruff. **'There's more to this than you know.'**

'Really?' I said. 'It doesn't look much like it to me.' Then –

'THIEF!' I spat.

The intruder leapt up.

He was ready to run.

So was I.

'No!' growled Gruff. **'Saucy, will you just listen!'**

He looked almost angry.

I glanced from one face to the other. There was something up, but what it could possibly be, I couldn't make out.

'All right,' I said quietly, 'I'm listening. But after that ... I'm chasing. Got it?'

Only, of course, after listening, I wasn't chasing anyone anywhere.

This straggly-looking animal wasn't a cat who should be hissed at and driven off. This wasn't a cat who was up to no good and should know better.

This was a cat who needed help.

'Right,' said Gruff when he'd finished telling the thief's story, **'now that we've got that sorted out – Saucy, I'd like you to say hello to Smart.'**

'Good to meet you,' said Smart. 'I've been seeing you around.'

'Where?' I asked. 'I've never seen you before in my life.'

'I'm pretty good at staying out of sight,' Smart replied. 'I have to be. But I've spotted you and your mates camping outside different cat flaps the last couple of nights. On the look-out for me, I should imagine.'

I was astonished. 'How could you have spotted us?' I gasped. 'We were incredibly well hidden.'

Smart shrugged. 'Just something else I've got pretty good at.'

We couldn't let Smart stay with us in the kitchen. It was beginning to get light. John and Sarah's dad was usually up early for work. It wouldn't do to let him find a stray cat in the house. Especially one who looked as though he might have four generations of fleas living in his fur.

'Come back tonight,' I said. 'There's got to be something we can do to help you.'

I was worried, though. As Smart slipped outside through the cat flap, we had no way of knowing if we'd ever see him again.

It occurred to me that there might have been a time when Gruff and I couldn't have cared less about a cat like Smart. We wouldn't have been interested in his story. All we'd have seen was a thieving moggy who had no business being in our house, and seen him off.

But it's an odd thing living with Sarah and John. Because they include God in everything they do – because they try to be the kind of people God wants them to be – they're different somehow. They're not always looking out just for themselves, they're looking out for other people. They find ways to care for others who need their help.

Don't get me wrong, they have their moments. Plenty of squabbles go on in this house. But they're still God's friends, which means they try to live His way.

Sarah has a poster on her bedroom wall. It has a picture of a butterfly resting on a flower with its wings open. Underneath is a verse from the Bible:

That's what happens when you ask Jesus to come into your life. You become brand new. You leave your old, selfish life behind and start to live a fresh life for God – just as a butterfly leaves its old life as a caterpillar to become a brand-new, beautiful creature.

My Sarah says that what you choose has an effect on the way you live. If you choose to do bad things, you can end up in all sorts of trouble. If you choose to be selfish and think only of what you want, in the end, it won't make you happy

But if you choose to live your life with God at the centre, He will be with you every day. He will show you how to make the most of the life He has given to you. And, like Gruff says, His Holy Spirit will help you to grow more like Jesus.

That's what's happening to Gruff and me. Meeting Smart has made me realise it's not enough just to make sure we're all right. It's not enough just to think about what we need and whether we've got everything we want. God expects so much more of us than that. It might not be easy for an independent-minded cat who's used to getting her own way, and having her own special spot on her favourite pillow. But God wants us to put others first. He wants us to love each other. So that's exactly what Gruff and I are going to do.

There's a cat out there in trouble.

Smart needs help.

And Gruff and me? We're going to do whatever it takes to make sure he gets it.

DAY 25
Gruff:

It was just like any other morning. I had breakfast – moist meaty chunks in delicious gravy with a sprinkling of biscuits. I had a good, long scratch – behind the right ear; under the chin; across the tummy.

'Stop that, Gruff,' snapped John's mum.

Nothing changes.

Then I had my morning rootle around the garden. I can't get behind the shed any more since John's dad blocked me out, but that's all right. I've found a pretty comfortable spot for a lie down behind the compost heap. I don't even miss sneaking into next door's garden now, not really. And I actually feel so much better since I gave back all the things I took.

I do sometimes wonder what Mr and Mrs Grant thought when they found all those bits and pieces lined up on their garden bench, carefully put there by the little girl who was staying with them. I don't know whether she told them that the small, grey dog from next door had given them to her and, if she did, whether or not they believed her. But they never came knocking. As far as I know they never so much as asked about it.

I was just making my way across the lawn back to the house, when a cat suddenly appeared on the fence beside me. It looked quite thin and scrawny and its coat was a little on the rough side, but someone had obviously given it a brush recently.

There was a gleam in its eye, too. A gleam that could only mean three things: good food, a comfy bed. And love. Lots of it.

'Just popped over to say thanks again,' said Smart.

'We didn't really do anything,' I answered. 'Mrs Allbright next door, she's the one who's given you a home. Sarah always says she's the best neighbour anyone could wish for, and she's obviously right. I don't suppose it would have worked with Mr and Mrs Grant the other side. But Saucy was sure that if you went and sat in Mrs Allbright's front porch, meowing and looking as if you hadn't eaten in a fortnight (which, let's face it, you barely have), she wouldn't be able to resist. Mrs Allbright's got the biggest heart of anyone she knows, Sarah says. And since her husband died, she's been all on her own. I reckon it'll be good for her to have someone else about the place, too.'

Smart was grinning. 'I can't get over it,' he purred. 'I had tuna for supper and salmon for breakfast. I've never eaten so well in my life. And as for grooming, it doesn't even seem to be a nuisance. Mrs Allbright loves it. I lie in her lap and she brushes and brushes. Says she's going to get out every last one of those tangles. I've got my own blanket now, too, and she's going to the pet shop later to buy me a proper cat bed. Talk about landing on your feet! And it's all thanks to you two.'

'Not at all,' I said. 'Just glad we were able to point you in the right direction.'

'But you did so much more than that,' said Smart. 'You did something for me no one else ever has. You listened. You didn't rush in and send me packing before I'd had a chance to explain. And when you knew I was in trouble, you cared about me. You cared about me enough to do something. You found me somewhere else to live. Do you know what that is, Gruff?

That's heroic.'

If you're going to stand up for God, that means people have got to see Him at work in your life. They've got to see that the way you live with God is different from the way others live who haven't made friends with Him yet. It isn't easy. It means you've got to try and do the right thing when it might seem much easier or more fun to do what's wrong. It means you need to try and show God's love to others in everything you do, even when it's difficult or you don't feel like it. Then maybe they'll be able to see how wonderful He is and they might want to get to know Him, too.

But if we ask Him, God will give us all the power we need to do just that.

I've never been called heroic before. At least not when I've been wide awake! And I've realised something. All those things I used to want to be – a stunt dog, a bodyguard, a thief-catcher – now, what I want more than anything is to be what God wants.

Because the truth is, being a hero for God ... well ... that's better than anything.

Collect the set:

You can always talk to God
Dave's Dizzy Doodles
ISBN: 978-1-85345-552-0

Confidently step out in faith
Danny's Daring Days
ISBN: 978-1-85345-502-5

Become a stronger person
John's Jam-packed Jottings
ISBN: 978-1-85345-503-2

Keep your friendships strong
Paul's Potty Pages
ISBN: 978-1-85345-456-1

You can show God's love to others
Josie's Jazzy Journal
ISBN: 978-1-85345-457-8

Christians needn't be boring
Benny's Barmy Bits
ISBN: 978-1-85345-431-8

You are special to God
Sarah's Secret Scribblings
ISBN: 978-1-85345-432-5

£5.99 each

IF YOU LIKED THIS BOOK, YOU'LL LOVE THESE:

TOPZ

An exciting, day-by-day look at the Bible for children aged from 7 to 11. As well as simple prayers and Bible readings every day, each issue includes word games, puzzles, cartoons and contributions from readers. Fun and colourful, *Topz* helps children get to know God.
ISSN: 0967-1307
£2.49 each (bimonthly)
£13.80 UK annual subscription (6 issues, includes p&p)

TOPZ FOR NEW CHRISTIANS

Thirty days of Bible notes to help 7- to 11-year-olds find faith in Jesus and have fun exploring their new life with Him.
ISBN: 978-1-85345-104-1
£2.49

TOPZ GUIDE TO THE BIBLE

A guide offering exciting and stimulating ways for 7- to 11- year-olds to become familiar with God's Word. With a blend of colourful illustrations, cartoons and lively writing, this is the perfect way to encourage children to get to know their Bibles.
ISBN: 978-1-85345-313-7
£2.99

Prices correct at time of printing and exclusive of p&p

National Distributors

UK: (and countries not listed below)
CWR, Waverley Abbey House, Waverley Lane, Farnham, Surrey GU9 8EP.
Tel: (01252) 784700 Outside UK (44) 1252 784700 Email: mail@cwr.org.uk

AUSTRALIA: KI Entertainment, Unit 21 317-321 Woodpark Road, Smithfield, New South Wales 2164. Tel: 1 800 850 777 Fax: 02 9604 3699
Email: sales@kientertainment.com.au

CANADA: David C Cook Distribution Canada, PO Box 98, 55 Woodslee Avenue, Paris, Ontario N3L 3E5. Tel: 1800 263 2664 Email: swansons@cook.ca

GHANA: Challenge Enterprises of Ghana, PO Box 5723, Accra.
Tel: (021) 222437/223249 Fax: (021) 226227 Email: ceg@africaonline.com.gh

HONG KONG: Cross Communications Ltd, 1/F, 562A Nathan Road, Kowloon.
Tel: 2780 1188 Fax: 2770 6229 Email: cross@crosshk.com

INDIA: Crystal Communications, 10-3-18/4/1, East Marredpalli, Secunderabad – 500026, Andhra Pradesh. Tel/Fax: (040) 27737145
Email: crystal_edwj@rediffmail.com

KENYA: Keswick Books and Gifts Ltd, PO Box 10242-00400, Nairobi.
Tel: (254) 20 312639/3870125 Email: keswick@swiftkenya.com

MALAYSIA: Salvation Book Centre (M) Sdn Bhd, 23 Jalan SS 2/64, 47300 Petaling Jaya, Selangor. Tel: (03) 78766411/78766797
Fax: (03) 78757066/78756360 Email: info@salvationbookcentre.com

Canaanland, No. 25 Jalan PJU 1A/41B, NZX Commercial Centre, Ara Jaya, 47301 Petaling Jaya, Selangor. Tel: (03) 7885 0540/1/2 Fax: (03) 7885 0545
Email: info@canaanland.com.my

NEW ZEALAND: KI Entertainment, Unit 21 317-321 Woodpark Road, Smithfield, New South Wales 2164, Australia. Tel: 0 800 850 777 Fax: +612 9604 3699
Email: sales@kientertainment.com.au

NIGERIA: FBFM, Helen Baugh House, 96 St Finbarr's College Road, Akoka, Lagos. Tel: (01) 7747429/4700218/825775/827264 Email: fbfm@hyperia.com

PHILIPPINES: OMF Literature Inc, 776 Boni Avenue, Mandaluyong City.
Tel: (02) 531 2183 Fax: (02) 531 1960 Email: gloadlaon@omflit.com

SINGAPORE: Alby Commercial Enterprises Pte Ltd, 95 Kallang Avenue #04-00, AIS Industrial Building, 339420. Tel: (65) 629 27238 Fax: (65) 629 27235
Email: marketing@alby.com.sg

SOUTH AFRICA: Struik Christian Books, 80 MacKenzie Street, PO Box 1144, Cape Town 8000. Tel: (021) 462 4360 Fax: (021) 461 3612
Email: info@struikchristianmedia.co.za

SRI LANKA: Christombu Publications (Pvt) Ltd, Bartleet House, 65 Braybrooke Place, Colombo 2. Tel: (9411) 2421073/2447665
Email: dhanad@bartleet.com

USA: David C Cook Distribution Canada, PO Box 98, 55 Woodslee Avenue, Paris, Ontario N3L 3E5, Canada. Tel: 1800 263 2664 Email: swansons@cook.ca

CWR is a Registered Charity – Number 294387
CWR is a Limited Company registered in England – Registration Number 1990308